David Patneaude

# SOMEONE WAS WATCHING

ALBERT WHITMAN & COMPANY
Morton Grove, Illinois

*Also by David Patneaude*

Dark Starry Morning

Library of Congress Cataloging-in-Publication Data

Patneaude, David
Someone was watching / David Patneaude.
p.   cm.
Summary:  When his baby sister disappears from the
river near their summer home, eighth grader Chris fights
the assumption that she has drowned and sets off on a
journey to discover the truth.
ISBN 0-8075-7531-3 (hardcover)
ISBN 0-8075-7532-1 (paperback)
[1. Missing persons—Fiction.  2. Kidnapping—Fiction.
3.  Mystery and detective stories.]
I. Title.
PZ7.P2734So    1993                    92-39130
[Fic]—dc20                             CIP
                                       AC

The text of this book is set in Bookman Light.
Design by Susan B. Cohn.

To Judy, Matt, Jaime, Jeff, for your love, support, and inspiration, and to Adam, a real-life hero.

**1**

**THE** trip started off better than Chris had expected. The day was bright and warm, with just a hint of the long shadows that would soon signal fall's arrival. And his parents actually spoke to each other at first, although the talk was forced and without laughter, the smiles rare and wistful.

But an hour into the drive, silence had taken over the conversation. His mother stared out the window at the fields and trees. His father kept his eyes on the road while he put a tape in the stereo. The soft sound of a saxophone floated back to Chris in the rear seat, reminding him of something that he couldn't identify, maybe just a feeling. A moment later his dad ejected the tape with a jab of his finger, as if turning off a memory. The only sound then was road noise: the murmur of the engine, the hiss of the tires, the wind whistling through half-closed windows. The occasional hum of a car passing in the opposite direction on the two-lane highway.

"What time do you think we'll get to the river, Dad?" His voice sounded louder than he'd intended, yet he still wasn't sure he'd been heard. He knew the answer, but he wanted a response, any kind of response. He waited, decided to forget it, then tried again anyway. "Dad?" he said, anxiously brushing back a stray wisp of his sand-colored hair.

His father glanced over his shoulder. "What time did we leave home, Chris?" he asked, the annoyance obvious in his voice.

"Eleven-thirty, about."

"It's always been a two-hour drive from Milwaukee. You figure it out."

Chris had gotten his response. He watched his mom turn and give his dad a look that said "Don't take it out on him," and his dad return it with a "Don't start on me." Then they went back to their private pain, ignoring each other, ignoring the purpose of the trip, ignoring the kid in the back seat. Chris slumped down in the corner, his head against the window, and closed his eyes.

The purpose of the trip was to return to the site of the Incident, as everyone called it now. To face up to the reality of it. To acknowledge that it had really happened. To exorcise the devils of grief that had haunted their souls for the past three months. But Chris figured the real reason was to humor Dr. Wilde, who had come up with the idea. After all, if you're going to pay someone for counseling, you should probably do what she suggests, even if it seems like a waste of time. Chris and his mom and dad were plenty aware of the reality of the situation. It had seeped into their lives like foul swamp water, filling the empty spaces and contaminating everything else. What they needed wasn't more reality; what they needed was a way to deal with it.

He tried to fall asleep but couldn't. He'd spent a lot of time sleeping lately. And when he wasn't sleeping, he tried to stay active. But these were the hardest times: when he was wide awake with nothing to do. And his thoughts were so loud.

He decided to think about something pleasant. Football. Football season was about to start, and this year he wanted to turn out for tight end. He knew there was some competition for that position, but he was bigger and faster than the other two guys were. And he was tired of being a regular lineman. He thought he had a chance. He just wanted to go out there and catch the ball and run over somebody— show the coaches what he could do.

And there was school. Not usually his favorite thing, but this year was different. This year he was going into eighth grade, and eighth-graders were the top class—the leaders—of middle school. He was anxious to try out that spot, to see what it felt like. And there was another—a bigger—reason: this year he *needed* to be there. He needed to be busy and to study and think and come up with answers to questions that *could* be answered. Not like the ones he'd had to face lately.

And there was always Pat. Good old dependable Pat: his best friend for as long as he could remember. The guy who always phoned him no matter what. When Chris didn't want to go anywhere or do anything, Pat would talk him into it, anyway. He'd have two tickets to a Brewers game, or an inside tip on what store had the best buys on baseball cards, or a rumor of a spot at the golf course where they could find lost balls by the bucketful. When he couldn't talk him into doing something, he'd wait a day and try again. When Chris didn't feel like talking, Pat would just come over and sit with him or throw the football around or go for a walk with him. Sometimes Chris didn't know why Pat had stuck with him through the long summer, but he had. And Chris was grateful. He wasn't sure how he would have handled the Incident otherwise.

The Incident. It seemed as if every train of thought huffed and puffed its way back to the Incident. He remembered it as if it were yesterday, or an hour ago. But it was three months now.

He thought back to the day it happened: the Saturday before Memorial Day weekend—a happy time. The first trip of the year to the river. Opening up the cabin for the summer, trips into town for a movie and ice cream, and exploring the shops. Boating and fishing and swimming and picnics at the park. And walks on the beach with Molly, her miniature hand in his, tugging him along, trying to make him go faster, to hurry to the water to feed the ducks or throw rocks or search for little turtles and fish and frogs in the shallows.

But that day, she had seemed content to stay on the grassy area that bordered the sandy beach. The holiday was a week away, and there weren't very many people in the park. No one was in the water. The day had grown warm by early afternoon when they finished their picnic lunch, but the water was still too cold for swimming or even comfortable wading.

Chris's mom and dad were sitting on the big plaid blanket, reading and watching Molly color in her coloring book. Chris felt himself getting sleepy and made up his mind to take the video camera and go for a walk. He thought he could get some shots of boats out on the river or maybe some snapping turtles poking their beaked heads out of the water. He decided to sneak off without letting Molly see him, so he made hand signals to his dad, who looked up from his book and nodded at him. Molly would have wanted to go. *Why hadn't he taken her?*

He got away unnoticed and wandered down to the beach. He videotaped a lone duck landing in the water, a boat pulling a hardy water skier, and a bullfrog diving from a log. Fresh out of live subjects, he slowly raised the lens toward the horizon, leisurely moving it from left to right, panning across the river's surface, the beach, the grass and trees. A cooperative squirrel ran out and got its picture taken stuffing food in its mouth.

Then the afternoon sun got to him. He lay down on the warm sand and dozed off for a few minutes. When he awoke he noticed some interesting clouds making their way across the sky. He decided to take some more shots, imagining the tape set to music. But he tired of that in a hurry, got up, and started back to the picnic area.

At first he noticed nothing, except that both of his parents had fallen asleep reading. His mom was flat on her back. His dad had his head propped up on his hand, but his eyes were closed and he was breathing deeply. Then it hit him like a low blow, driving his breath out of him and triggering instant nausea.

"Dad! Mom!" he shouted, staggering toward them. They were awake, sitting up, looking at him with bewildered eyes. "Where's Molly?" he yelled at them.

"Molly?" his dad said, the color draining from his face. "She was just here. Just a minute ago."

"How would you know, Mike? You were asleep," his mom said, spitting the words out as if they were sour pills. They were both on their feet.

"So were you, Lynn," his dad shot back. His eyes, wild-animal eyes now, widened as he scanned the shoreline.

"But you said you'd keep an eye on her." Her voice was more a plea, a prayer, than a complaint.

His dad gave her a look instead of an answer. "You check the picnic area and parking lot," he said to her. "We'll check the beach."

"Hurry," his mom said.

Chris and his dad headed for the water, shouting Molly's name, asking the few people they passed if they had seen her. No one had. Chris heard his mom calling for Molly from the other side of the park. Panic had crept into her voice, pushing it to a higher, wavering pitch.

His dad started jogging along the shoreline to the north, peering into the dark water. Chris followed him for a moment, but then turned around. "I'm going to look in the other direction!" he shouted at his dad's back, and headed south. *The dock*, he thought. *She loves going out on the dock.*

The dock was a long, floating wood structure anchored to the beach on one end. The park workers took it out of the water every fall before the river iced over and put it back in place in the spring. It was located at the far south end of the beach, around the bend and out of sight. Chris lengthened his stride, kicking up puffs of sand as he accelerated toward it.

He rounded the curve and glanced at the dock. Nothing—not even a sun bather or fisherman. But he continued. Maybe she was playing in the sand on the other side, crouched down too low to see.

In a moment he was there. But he was alone. Lots of footprints, big and little, dotted the sand on the far side, but none he could recognize, none that looked small and fresh and playful. He stared into the shallow water where the dock met the beach, slowly lifting his gaze until he was looking along the length of the dock at the slow-moving, dark water beyond its other end. The river, nearly a mile wide here, was undisturbed by anything floating on its surface—except for two dark heads bobbing slowly up and down twenty feet from the end of the dock. Snapping turtles. His mom and dad would never let him swim when the big, beak-jawed turtles were visible in the river. There were tales of them pulling kids under, tales he'd never quite believed but was unwilling to challenge. He shuddered and stepped up on the dock, shouting Molly's name. From far away he could hear his dad's voice yelling for her. She hadn't been found.

Something moved on the end of the dock. Chris walked quickly toward it, scanning the water on both sides of him. It moved again, slow and colorful, pushed by the gentle breeze. The pages of a book, turning themselves over. He got closer, and his heart climbed into his throat. Tears blurred his vision but he'd already seen what it was. Molly's coloring book. He turned and ran toward the beach.

If the first part of that day seemed like a pleasant dream now, the rest of it was a nightmare, a dark merry-go-round on fast forward. The feelings had stuck with him; they wouldn't go away. And the events were intermingled; it was hard to remember one without the others.

He'd found his dad and then his mom. She called the police, and by the time she and Chris returned to the dock, his dad was frantically flailing through the icy water, diving and surfacing, diving and surfacing. His mom plunged in on the other side. Chris was about to follow her, but his dad told him to wade in the shallow water closer to shore.

Then the police came. And divers. And para-medics. And regular people who just wanted to help. And people who were curious. And newspaper and radio and television reporters. Big news in a little town.

But they didn't find her. The police searched and questioned, the divers rowed and dove. The para-medics walked the dock and beach, hanging close, waiting, hoping for a chance to work a miracle. His mom and dad tried to help but mostly wandered around, at first calling for Molly and talking to the search party, but then growing silent. And Chris prayed harder than he ever had before. He'd heard of a kid who had been under cold water for a long time and been revived. But the day wore on, and toward evening he quit praying. He could tell by looking at the faces of his mom and dad and the search party that they didn't expect to find her alive.

He sat on the dock and watched the divers continue to work back and forth between the end of the dock and the shore, slowly making their way downriver. He waited for them to bring her up, hoping now that they wouldn't. When it got too dark to see, they came ashore. They left, along with everyone else, promising to return the next day. Chris and his parents went back to the summer house for the night. No one slept.

Fewer people showed up the next day. A lot of folks were in church, someone said—praying. But they didn't find Molly. Not the divers, not the search party, not the dogs that they'd brought in to help. By evening the police said they were calling off the search. Chris heard them say that the river was still powerful with run-off this time of year and she could be miles downstream. His mom and dad didn't argue with the decision.

That night they returned to the summer house, packed, shut everything off, locked everything up, and drove to the city. They hadn't been back since.

Now they were going back, but not because anyone really wanted to. Dr. Wilde thought they should, so they were. But it wasn't going to be fun.

The car took a curve fast, shifting Chris's weight away from the window. He put his hand on the seat to balance himself, touching the indentation in the fabric where Molly's car seat had once been. He let his hand rest there for a moment. The dent was getting smaller. In a few months it would be gone.

**2**

**THEY** turned off the main highway onto the road to Greenwater. There was a more direct route to the summer house, but this detour had always been part of the ritual of coming to the beach. Chris was surprised that his dad had chosen to take it today. He figured that everyone would be anxious to get this trip over with.

"Need gas," his dad grunted, as if reading his mind.

In less than a minute they entered the little town. His dad drove into its only gas station.

"Can I get an ice cream?" Chris asked. He needed to take a walk.

"Sure, Chris," his mom said. "We'll pick you up on the way out."

"You guys want anything?" he asked.

"No, thanks," his mom said, turning toward him, but eyeing Chris's dad. "Mike?" she said after a moment. Her voice was soft but clear in the quiet of the car. At last his dad shook his head no. He was still shaking his head when Chris got out of the car, as if he were saying no to something else.

Chris crossed the street and walked back in the direction they'd come into town. He hadn't been to The Cloverbud since the accident. An ice cream cone would taste good. But when he reached the little shop, he saw that it was closed up and dark inside. A CLOSED sign hung in the window, almost on end, with the C pointing skyward. Bud and Clover must have taken the afternoon off. He walked next door to Village Books, and that was closed, too. He peered through the window, scratching his head. It must have been a real slow morning in Greenwater.

The next store down was Cowbutter Cookies. Chris breathed a sigh of relief. It was open. "I thank you, my stomach thanks you," he said to no one in particular as he walked in the door. Helen, the short, square-bodied woman behind the counter, looked up and smiled.

"Chris, how you doin'?" she asked. "How's the family? I haven't seen you guys in months." Her face went blank for a moment and then reddened. She pressed her lips together. Too late—the words had already popped out. They were hanging in the air, casting shadows on the conversation.

"We haven't been down since, uh, May," Chris replied.

"We were so sorry about Molly," she said. "She was a little doll. Frank was in the search party that day, you know."

Chris remembered Helen's husband being there. Combing the park, searching the beach, exploring the cold water, and emerging in long, dripping-wet pants to trudge along the shoreline again. He'd been one of the last ones to leave, and when he did there were tears in his eyes.

"I saw Frank there," Chris said. "He was a big help."

"I guess everybody did what they could. But that's a nasty piece of water for little kids. She's not the first one that's not been found, you know."

Chris knew. He'd heard the stories of other drownings. They'd just never meant much before.

"I'd like a couple of cookies," he said, steering the topic away from one that was getting old in a hurry. "A peanut butter for me and a chocolate chip for my friend."

"Your friend? Why didn't you bring him in with you?"

Chris stuck out his flat stomach, patting it fondly. "I did. He was too hungry to wait outside."

Helen smiled. "Still the comedian, huh, Chris?" She reached under the counter, grabbed a bag, and carefully stacked four big cookies in it. "These are on me today, but you've got to promise to come back sooner next time. And bring your folks in, too."

"Thanks. I will." He started for the door, feeling cheered and hungry.

But his parents drove up to the curb just as he walked outside, and when he got into the car the tension was still there. "The Cloverbud was closed," he said. "And Helen asked about you. She said to come in and see her next time we're in town."

"That may be a while, Chris," his dad said.

Was he supposed to ask why now?

No—his mom spoke up before he had to. "We've decided to sell the summer house, Chris," she said. Her voice was unsteady and she turned away from him, leaving him staring at the back of her head. Her shoulder-length brown hair danced in the breeze from the window.

He didn't say anything at first. He just wondered how the decision had been made. They hadn't even asked him. "Can't we wait?" he asked. "Maybe in a year or two we'll feel better about things. And then it would be too late."

"We can look for another house," his dad said. "We might even find one we like better."

"There's no place I'll like better," Chris said.

Neither of his parents said anything. He guessed that they were done discussing it. He slumped down in the seat, opening the bag of cookies. He was going to enjoy at least one of them before the knot in his stomach got too tight.

They took a right turn onto the main highway and headed toward the river. Chris rolled down his window. He could smell it now, even from a mile away: that late summer odor of algae blooming in the calm backwaters and shallows, and the faint fishy smell that was only noticeable at first approach to the water.

Memories of other summers came flooding back to him. He thought about the years before Molly had been born, when it had been just the three of them. They'd had a lot of fun coming to the river. Sometimes he'd come alone with his parents, and sometimes he'd bring Pat or another friend along. It had all seemed so natural. He'd never really regretted not having a little brother or sister because he'd never had one.

His mom and dad had talked about the possibility of having another kid when he was younger, but he'd pretty much dismissed the idea. Then, four summers ago they'd taken him out for dinner and told him that his mom was pregnant. He was shocked, but he didn't think he'd ever seen bigger smiles on their faces.

She was born on Christmas Eve, only the first of many times that she disrupted his formerly peaceful, predictable life. His dad gave out little Christmas stockings full of candy and called her his sweet surprise. His mom simply refused to put her down.

It wasn't long before she was winning Chris over, too. He found himself volunteering to hold her and creeping into her room to check on her at night. And once the weather warmed up, walking to the beach with her in the backpack. There, he'd throw rocks or feed the ducks and she'd make noises over his shoulder. Ten-year-old girls thought she was adorable, which was a nice extra incentive. And except for once or twice, his friends didn't tease him about spending time with his baby sister.

By her second summer, she was talking. She said "shoot" when she watched him play basketball in the backyard, and "bite" when she begged him for some of whatever he happened to be eating at the time. She called him Kis. She would run to meet him whenever she heard him come home, yelling, "Kis! Kis!" He was never quite sure when she was saying his name and when she wanted a kiss. So he'd pick her up and give her a kiss just to make sure. At the summer house, he took her wading in the river and taught her to help him feed the ducks. At first she wasn't sure about those greedy little creatures with the hard mouths, but Chris told her he had too many customers to handle all by himself. Before long, her favorite thing was feeding her "custards."

In the next two years, she was transformed from a baby to a little girl. Chris had had a hard time believing how fast she was growing up. At the time of the accident, his parents had planned to start her in part-time preschool in the fall. Chris figured she was ready. She was already trying to read books to him. Of course, her "reading" consisted of reciting from memory what was on each page of her favorite picture books. But she was good at it, good enough that she'd catch anyone who tried to skip over anything when they were reading to her.

*If she were sitting in the back seat of the car with me now, I'd be glad to read her as many books as she wanted,* Chris thought. *And I wouldn't skip a word.*

They turned left at the River Road stop sign, drove a quarter of a mile north, and turned left again into their driveway. Across the road the big river moved as slowly as the midday sun, so slowly it couldn't be distinguished from a giant puddle. Its surface was pool-table smooth, dimpled only occasionally by a rising fish, a duck, or something else: a turtle's head?

Chris looked at the house. It was different somehow. He'd expected the grass to be long, and it was. And the flowerbeds needed weeding. But the house itself had changed. He'd always thought its front, with its big picture windows on either side of the red door, looked like a smiling, surprised face. Now it stared out blankly, as if wondering what was going on. Maybe it was because the blinds were closed. But it made Chris uneasy. What if the house knew that it was going to be sold to someone else after all these years?

They went inside, into the lifeless, musty air. Dust clung to everything. His mom opened the windows and sat down on the couch with her face in her hands. His dad walked over to her, stood there for a moment, and went into the kitchen. Chris heard the faucet running and the back door close. He walked into his bedroom and flopped onto the bed. Dust particles mushroomed up into the air and danced in the sunlight above him. He stared through them at the small, familiar stain on the ceiling. It had always reminded him of an ice cream cone, half-melted and broken.

He heard the lawnmower putt to a start and decided to go help. He walked out through the living room. His mom stood at the window, staring at the river. She was thinner than he'd ever seen her, and he noticed for the first time today that she wasn't wearing makeup. She looked sad and lost and vulnerable.

"I'm going to help Dad," he said.

"Okay, honey," she said, smiling at him. "I'll be out to give you guys a hand in a little while. I just need to do a few things in here first." Her brown eyes glistened. Her smile faded to a quivering crease on her face.

Chris stepped outside. Through the window he watched his mom walk to the fireplace and begin taking down pictures from the mantel—pictures of a family at their summer place.

He grabbed a shovel and attacked the flower bed next to the door, ripping out bulky clumps of weeds and warm dirt. Sweat beaded on his forehead and trickled into his eyes, mixing with tears and continuing down his cheeks.

For the next two hours Chris lost himself in his work. When he finally stopped and looked around, the yard had changed. Between the three of them, they'd gotten it close to the way he remembered it. The lawn was trimmed and the flowers stood tall and free of weeds. Fresh-cut grass filled his nose with a familiar smell and his mind with memories.

Chris watched his dad remove a board and a small toolbox from the trunk of the car. He walked over to the white picket fence that bordered the front of the yard and nailed it to a post facing the street. Chris couldn't read it, but he knew what it said. He recognized a FOR SALE sign, even from the back. Without looking at Chris or his mom, his dad returned to the car, put the toolbox in the trunk, and started for the house. "I'm going for a run," he mumbled as he hurried up the steps.

Five minutes later he was back outside in his running clothes. He glanced at his watch and headed down the driveway toward the street, breaking into a fast jog.

"Can we go to the park when you get back?" Chris's mom called after him.

"Sure, Lynn," he said. "Give me an hour." He took a left and headed down the road.

Chris watched him until he disappeared around the bend. He'd been a runner as long as Chris could remember, but now he seemed to run differently. Head down. Mechanical. Finding no pleasure but willing to take on the pain.

A long time ago he'd told Chris that running gave him a chance to think about things and develop ideas. Chris wondered what he was thinking about now, what kinds of ideas he was developing.

**3**

**THEY** arrived at the park an hour and a half later. It was a nice walk from the house, just a half mile down the road. The day was still warm and sunny, but it was approaching dinnertime and a lot of people had already left or were getting ready to leave. They would have plenty of space to themselves. But Chris wasn't sure if that was good or bad.

They walked past their usual spot, the place where they'd been on the day of the drowning, and found a secluded grassy area half-circled by leafy trees. Splotches of shade offered some shelter from the warm sun.

"This is a nice little location," his dad said, shaking out the big plaid blanket and smoothing it out on the ground.

*Always the salesman*, Chris thought. "I liked the old one better," he said. His mom looked at him. She seemed ready to say something, but instead cleared her throat and stared out at the river.

"This will do fine," his dad said and sat down on a corner of the blanket as if to say that he wasn't about to move. Chris and his mom each chose another corner. His dad shoved the picnic basket to the middle.

His mom cleared her throat again. "I don't know if I've ever seen the river this green," she said.

His dad looked up, studying the water. "Eighty-four," he said. "It was greener in eighty-four. That was a real hot summer."

Chris thought back on the summers he'd spent here. As far as he could remember, they'd all been warm. The river had always turned green.

For several minutes no one spoke. Was this going to be the extent of the conversation, then? Picnic spots and green water? The knot in Chris's stomach wasn't going away. And this pointless small talk was just making it worse. He took a deep breath, sucking in the moist air, and swallowed hard. "So, are we going to talk about it?" he asked, staring at the blanket.

"What's that, Chris?" his mom asked. He watched her eyes squeeze shut as if she were trying to keep something out.

"You know. Molly and the accident and our feelings about it and how we feel about each other and what we're going to do about everything. The reason Dr. Wilde told us to come here."

"We will," his dad said. "We will."

"Now," Chris said. "We need to do it now." He watched his mom's shoulders sag. "We didn't come here to put stupid FOR SALE signs on our house or talk about how green the stupid river was in 1984."

His dad looked over at his mom and then at Chris. "You start, Chris," he said finally. "Tell us what's on your mind, everything you can think of. By then your mom or I will be ready to talk. Okay?"

Chris nodded. He hadn't planned on going first, and he didn't want to make a speech. But he wanted badly to have their lives back to normal or at least better than they were now, and he was willing to try anything.

He wasn't sure how to express himself or how his parents would react. Then he found some words.

"I told everybody this when we were at Dr. Wilde's," he said, just above a whisper, "but it keeps going around in my head: I don't understand why it happened. That's still the hardest thing. And not being able to do anything about it. Why did it have to be Molly? Why *our* family? It doesn't make sense. We're good people. Why didn't it happen to some bad people? I can't stand thinking about her at the bottom of the river, what she must've felt when she fell in. Can you imagine it?" The expressions on his parents' faces told him that they could. That they had.

"Trying to breathe and not being able to," he continued. "How scared she must've been. The pain. The cold. The darkness."

"I know your feelings, Chris," his mom said. Her voice cracked and tore at him. He looked at her tear-filled eyes. He could feel his dad's gaze.

"Every day," his dad said. "Every hour. Every minute I'm awake. I see her face and wonder what might have been." He stared down at the blanket and then out toward the river. Shadows on the ground were lengthening.

Chris held his breath. He didn't want the smell of the river—the smell of decay—in his nose. Not right now. He swallowed again. "One thing I haven't said before—maybe it's the reason things aren't getting any easier—is that I blame myself a lot of the time. Why did I have to walk away and leave her there just so I could take stupid pictures? I thought about taking her with me. Why didn't I? She'd still be alive now." He paused and took a quick breath, trying to ignore the smell. His mom and dad were both shaking their heads.

"And I'm sorry, but I blame you guys, too. I mean, why did you have to fall asleep, Dad? You were supposed to be watching her." His dad's face suddenly looked old. "And why were *you* sleeping, Mom? You know he can't stay awake after he eats a big lunch." She stared straight into Chris's eyes as if welcoming whatever it was he wanted to say. She nodded, encouraging him to go on. "And why wasn't she wearing her life jacket? What good did it do her sitting back in the car?" He paused again and sat there, looking back and forth at his parents. "It's hard to go on like this, just kind of ignoring what happened, or at least what we feel about it. I think so, anyway."

He felt tired, as if he'd pedaled his bike up a long hill on a muggy August afternoon. Only now there was another hill to worry about: how were his mom and dad going to react?

But they didn't get angry. They didn't try to defend themselves or launch an attack on Chris's feelings or what he'd said. They sat on the blanket and looked at him for a long time, and then at each other.

His mom finally began talking. She covered some familiar things—things she'd mentioned during their counseling sessions—but then she talked about the day of the accident, how she had blamed Chris's dad for what had happened but knew all along that it wasn't his fault. She talked about her own feelings of guilt, how she wished she could go back and do things differently, how much she loved Molly, and how she longed for their lives to get back to normal.

She took Chris's hand and told him never to

blame himself and thanked him for talking to them about his feelings. Her face was damp with tears when she stopped and looked over at Chris's dad.

His dad stared out at the river. He didn't say anything. Chris watched him swallow hard and run his hand nervously through his dark hair. For a long moment, Chris thought that maybe he wouldn't talk. Maybe he'd just sit there and wait for someone else to start talking again. Maybe he was just waiting for it to get dark so they could go home and forget this discussion ever happened.

But then he began. His voice was soft and shaky at first, like Chris's used to be when he had to talk in front of the class. But then it smoothed out, got stronger. Maybe he sensed that Chris and his mom were really willing to listen, that all the anger wasn't directed at him. He said something he'd never admitted before: that he blamed himself for the whole thing. All he had had to do was stay awake, he said, just stand up when he started feeling tired. It never would have happened. And that he was pretty much in charge of Molly's life jacket. He'd left it in the car. He didn't think she'd really need it with her whole family there. He knew he'd never take his eyes off her. But he did, and now she was gone. And he hadn't been able to deal with the fact that she wasn't coming back. And that it was his fault, and that he'd wrecked their lives and their family relationship, and he didn't know what to do about it, but he wanted to do something to make things better again.

He held out his hands to Chris and Chris's mom. They took them and slid from their corners of the blanket to his. And they hugged, and breathed words of comfort, their voices mixing together and floating away on an early evening breeze. Tears ran freely down their cheeks and onto each other's cheeks and shoulders. While the sun set and the air cooled and the park emptied of people, they sat on their blanket, holding each other, vowing to face their trouble together, beat it, and get on with their lives.

Finally, Chris stood up and walked toward the river. His legs felt like dry spaghetti, weak and stiff. But inside he felt good, better than he could remember feeling in a long time.

He waded into the river and stood knee deep. Sand filled the spaces between his toes. The warm water left little green blooms of algae on his skin as he gazed across its surface. He hadn't touched the river since the day Molly had died. It didn't seem as threatening now, not as cold or dark or deep as it had then. And he didn't hate it as much anymore. He didn't wish it would dry up or turn into a big ribbon of cement winding through the state. But he still couldn't help wishing that he had that day to live over again.

He looked back toward shore, into the orange

glare of the setting sun. Through squinted eyes, he saw his mom and dad waving to him. He waved back and they stood up together. The sun's rays filtered through the trees and lit their hair afire, turning their faces into dark shadows beneath the light. His heart skipped, and a cold tingle ran down the back of his neck. But then they stepped toward him, and he saw their smiles. He hurried from the water.

They walked back home single file on the road's narrow shoulder. A comfortable weariness had come down on them like a heavy, warm blanket. They didn't say much, but Chris felt that they were together again.

"I've got something I need to do," his dad said when they reached their driveway.

Chris and his mom watched as he retrieved the hammer from the trunk of the car and pried the FOR SALE sign from the post. He bowed deeply to their applause and sailed the sign into the trunk with a flourish. "Maybe we'll need that for something else some day," he said. Chris slammed the trunk lid shut, and they walked into the house.

On his way to bed later, Chris glanced at the mantel. The photographs were back.

**4**

**DESPITE** going to bed early and sleeping late, Chris felt exhausted on the trip home the next day. He tried reading and dozed off. He tried looking at the scenery and dozed off. When he awoke, his mom was asleep and his dad had his window rolled down and the radio turned up, sure signs that he, too, was fighting sleep. Five minutes later, they pulled into a rest area, and his mom took over the driving duties. Chris and his dad were both asleep before they'd gone a mile farther down the highway.

When Chris woke up again they were pulling into their driveway. His mom braked the car in front of the garage and turned off the ignition. It was suddenly quiet.

"The house looks nice," his mom said, resting her

hand on his dad's shoulder.

"It's good to be home," his dad said. He stretched back over the seat and tousled Chris's hair.

Chris ducked and scrambled out the door. He stood by the side of the car, grinning, hoping his dad would chase him. He was ready.

But his dad got out and just looked at him for a long moment. "I like your hair like that, Chris," he said finally, a smile in his eyes. "It reminds me of when you were a little kid."

Chris felt the top of his head. His hair was sticking straight up.

"Back when you were still cute," his dad said.

Chris knew he was kidding, but he remembered when his dad and mom used to tell him what a cute kid he was. He hadn't heard it for a long time.

"You still think I was a cute kid?" he asked.

"None cuter," his mom said, getting out of the car. Suddenly she got that funny, faraway look in her eyes that Chris had seen too often in the past few months. He knew she was thinking about another cute kid.

His dad must have seen the look, too. "How could you miss with such good-looking parents, Chris?" he said with a smile. He turned to Chris's mom. "We passed our good looks on to both of our kids, didn't we, honey?" he said. Chris felt relieved. His dad wasn't going to ignore what everyone was feeling.

His mom smiled. *Bittersweet,* Chris thought, understanding the word as he never had before. She looked at him and through him. "We sure did," she said, slipping an arm around his dad's waist.

"I'm glad you think so," Chris said.

He grabbed his bag and headed for the house. When he got there, he found a piece of paper taped to the front door. Curious, he took it off, unfolded it, and looked at some familiar handwriting. It was a note from Pat.

> Chris—
> I came by to see if you were home yet.
> You weren't. Hope everything went okay
> at the river. Call me when you get back.
> Pat.

"From Pat?" his mom asked, reaching the front step.

"Yeah," Chris said. "I'm supposed to give him a call."

His dad unlocked the door and nudged it open. "I think you should," he said. Chris rushed through and was almost to the phone before his dad called after him. "But before you make any plans, Chris, your mom and I thought it would be good to look at the tape tonight. What do you think?"

The tape. Now that this was out in the open they weren't about to sweep it back under the rug, Chris decided. He knew what tape they were talking about.

He hadn't forgotten it. As far as he knew, it was still in the camera. He stared at the phone for a moment before answering them, trying to think of what might be on the tape. Trying to think if he wanted to see it. He decided he did.

"Sounds like a good idea to me," he said. "Okay if Pat comes over for it, too?" He couldn't see their faces, but for a moment he heard the silence of their exchanged glances.

Then his dad's voice: "He might as well. He's just about one of the family."

Then his mom: "And ask him to come for dinner, Chris. Tell him spaghetti. Lots of it."

"Thanks," Chris said, picking up the phone. Now he hoped Pat could come, and would want to. He figured he'd need the company.

**5**

**PAT** decided to come over early—real early. Five minutes after their phone conversation, Chris looked out his upstairs bedroom window and saw him run into the front yard. He was doing his impersonation of a running back, dodging and faking and hurdling phantom defenders as he crossed the lawn. One hand cradled an imaginary football, while the other warded off would-be tacklers. Chris smiled, but didn't laugh. At nearly six feet and 170 pounds, with sprinter's speed, Pat looked as if he belonged on a football field. And he did. Like Chris, he'd played junior football since he was eight years old.

Chris hurried downstairs, listening for the doorbell, half expecting Pat to crash right in. But he didn't hear anything, and when he opened the door, he saw why: Pat was doing his touchdown dance on the lawn, his back to the house. Chris let him go through his whole routine, including the ceremonial spiking of the imaginary ball, before letting him know he had a real audience.

"Nice moves, hot dog," Chris said. "They never laid a hand on you. But the ref just dropped his penalty flag."

Pat turned slowly, a sheepish grin on his face. "You better be practicing your dance, too, Chris," he said. "You know you're gonna be getting some TDs this year."

"If we have anyone to throw me the ball," Chris said. His team wasn't known for its passing attack.

"Hey, if we don't have anyone else that can do it, I'll get back there and toss you a few."

"I won't hold my breath," Chris said. But Pat could probably do it, and the coaches would probably let him.

"You coming in?" Chris said.

"Yeah," Pat said, walking toward the door. He gave Chris a playful punch to the shoulder—a playful punch that Chris felt all the way down to his bones. "How ya doin', big guy?" Pat said. "How was your weekend?"

"Better than I figured it would be," Chris said. He thought for a moment while they walked into the house and he closed the door behind them. "A lot better than I figured it would be."

"Really?" Pat said, looking Chris in the eye. "It really went okay?"

"My mom and dad are talking again," Chris said quietly. He glanced around, not sure where they were, but they didn't appear to be in hearing range, at least. "They're even talking to each other."

"That's great," Pat said. "That's great." He made a throwing motion and then repeated it. "You wanna go out and toss the football around for a while?"

"The real one?"

"The real one. You can even practice your dance."

"It's a deal," Chris said.

Chris was near starvation when they sat down to dinner, but by the time he was halfway through his spaghetti, Pat's plate was already empty. Pat, who had started out with a mountain of a serving, sat with his fork in his hand and a silly look on his face, as if he were waiting for a load of pasta to fall from the sky.

"I think The Solution to America's Food Surplus needs another helping," Chris said.

His mom, who had barely started on her food, looked over at Pat and his clean plate, smiled, and shook her head. "Would you like some more, Pat?" she said.

"I thought you'd never ask," he said, handing her his plate.

"Why don't you just bring the whole pot over for him?" Chris's dad said.

Chris and Pat did the dishes and shuffled into the dimly lit family room where Chris's mom was removing the tape from the video camera. She handed it to his dad, who put it into the recorder.

"You guys ready for this?" he said.

They nodded and found chairs to sit in while Chris's dad started the tape and sat down on the couch with his mom.

The television screen flickered on and Chris focused in on it. Everything else in the room blurred and faded out. The TV was nothing but gray fuzz and buzzing for what seemed like a month. He wondered if the whole tape were blank and whether or not he'd be disappointed if it were. He didn't think he would. Maybe something had been wrong with the camera that day. Maybe there was something else they could watch instead—anything else. But then his mom's face came on the screen, and his dad's voice tumbled out of the speaker: "Tell us what day it is, hon."

"It's May 20th," his mom said, "and we're on our way to the river for a weekend of fun and sun. Greenwater, here we come!"

The picture faded out and right back in again. And there was Molly, walking through the front door holding Chris's hand. As they approached the driveway, the camera zoomed in on her, showing her face in closeup, her blond hair aglow in the morning sun. She was looking up at Chris with a serious expression on her face. Her voice floated out of the TV as if she were right in the room. "I want to sit in Daddy's seat, Kis. I want to drive to the river."

"When you're bigger, Molly," Chris's voice said.

The picture faded out, and then she was back on the screen again, sitting in the driver's seat with her hands on the steering wheel, smiling at the camera through the open window. "I'm driving the car," she said with a big smile.

"Where are you driving, Molly?" his mom's voice said.

"I'm driving to the river," Molly said. "Far away to the big river. To our little house."

In the next scene she was in the back of the car with Chris, sitting in her car seat and looking grumpily through the back window. Her plans had been spoiled. But she smiled and waved at the camera when Chris asked her to.

Then they were on the road. Pictures taken through the car window of the countryside between home and the river flashed on the screen. Road noise and music and voices paraded from the speaker. Chris picked Molly's small voice out of the jumble, trying to sing along with a song on the radio. He closed his eyes and imagined she was there in the room. Her voice stopped and he opened his eyes again. Her face filled the screen. Chris had caught her sleeping in her seat, her head flopped to the side, her long eyelashes resting on her round cheeks.

Then she was gone again. They'd arrived in Greenwater and his dad was operating the camera, doing his traditional scene of Chris's mom walking out of the women's room at the gas station. On every trip they took he had to have at least one of these shots. He called it his contribution to art. Chris's mom called it childish. Once she even crawled out of a restroom window to escape the camera. But she usually managed to laugh with the rest of the family when the segment showed up on the TV screen.

Now, she was walking out once more, this time holding Molly's hand. Molly could never decide to go the first time she had a chance to. She was looking up at her mom and talking while they walked toward the camera. "*Now* can we get ice cream, Mom?" she asked. "*Now* can we?"

The next scenes ran together like a steady stream of cold rain drops on Chris's head. Molly and Chris walking into The Cloverbud for ice cream and wandering back out with Bud and Clover and an ice cream cone the size of a small building in Molly's hand. More scenery between town and the summer house. And scenes at the house: Chris and his dad throwing the football in the front yard, his mom pointing out the famous tree—the tree with the six-inch trunk—that Chris tried to hide behind once to avoid taking some medicine. Molly helping to mow the lawn with her toy lawnmower.

Then they were at the beach: Molly in her little flowery swimsuit trying to catch a big plastic ball; Molly and Chris racing each other through the sand; Molly winning and squealing with delight and running ankle deep through the cold water; Molly and Chris and their dad eating lunch on the blanket; Molly feeding leftover bread to a squirrel.

The river scenes started—the ones Chris taped after he wandered down to the beach by himself. He knew he'd seen the last of Molly, but he kept watching the screen, transfixed by the motion and color and dim noises in the background. A bird, a water skier, a splash far out in the river. Sand and grass and trees and sunshine. A quiet day in late spring.

Then the screen was blank, and the only sound from the speaker was the buzz of dead static. Chris kept staring at the fuzzy gray image in front of him, vaguely aware of Pat getting up and moving toward the door.

"I gotta go, big guy," Pat whispered. "Talk to you tomorrow." And he was gone.

Too late, Chris waved his hand and said, "See ya, Pat." The effort dragged him out of his trance. He glanced around the room. His mom and dad, sound asleep, leaned on each other in the middle of the sofa.

He stood, stretched, and walked stiffly over to them. He gently shook his dad's shoulder but got no response. "Dad. Mom," he said in a tired voice. But they didn't move. He pulled a big knit blanket from underneath the coffee table, draped it carefully over them, and started upstairs, switching off the TV and VCR on the way.

Sometime during the night he awoke with his mom and dad standing over his bed. Dim light streamed through his open door from the hall.

"You okay, Chris?" his dad asked.

"You were talking in your sleep," his mom said.

For a minute Chris couldn't think. "I'm okay," he finally said. But he didn't feel okay. He felt troubled— burdened—but he didn't know why.

"Well, sleep tight, then," his dad said and put his hand on Chris's head.

His mom kissed his cheek, and they walked out and closed the door, leaving Chris sweating in the warm room.

Then he remembered his dream. The warm wind in his face, the trees drifting by like ships' sails, the exhaustion, the silence in the car. Then the voice on the radio, sounding just as it had during the trip back home from the summer place last May. The flat, uncaring voice trying to sound concerned. "Missing and presumed drowned," it had said. Missing and presumed drowned. He got out of bed and staggered to the bathroom for a drink.

He didn't feel better when he got back to his room. It wasn't just a dream he could forget; it was a memory that would play in his mind forever. And something else was gnawing at him, too, but he couldn't figure out what it was. He sat on the edge of his bed and thought, but nothing shook loose. Whatever was stuck was stuck tight. Finally he crawled back under the covers and fell asleep, tossing fitfully back and forth across the mattress.

When he opened his eyes again it was still dark. The only light in his room shone from his clock radio. He turned on his side to look at it—3:21. Early. Real early. He didn't even get up that early to go fishing. But he was wide awake, and something was playing through his mind. Something troubling.

The videotape. Scenes and sounds from the videotape were rolling through the built-in player in his head. But they were fuzzy and he couldn't play them back. He couldn't reverse and fast forward and stop them in their tracks.

He lay on his back and tried to think. Had he just been dreaming, or had a bit of reality crept into his dreams? He couldn't sort it out. He had to go downstairs and see.

The family room was dark. Chris switched on a table lamp to low power, blinked his eyes to get used to the light, and turned on the TV and VCR. He picked up the remote control and sat down on the rug six feet in front of the screen. After rewinding the tape, he hit the play button and the familiar images reappeared. Once again, his family was in the front yard getting ready to leave for the river. But this wasn't what he wanted to see. He hit the fast forward button and stopped. Country scenes taken from the car window. Fast forward. Stop. His mom coming out of the restroom. Fast forward. Stop. He and Molly walking into the Cloverbud. Fast forward. Stop. At the summer house. Fast forward. Stop. At the beach. Fast forward. Stop. His shots down at the water. Stop. *This* was what he needed to see.

He reversed the tape a bit to make sure he wouldn't miss anything and then let it play. Molly was feeding the squirrel again for just a moment, and then she was gone and the camera lens was scanning slowly along the river's surface. Following a lone duck landing in the water and a water skier, stopping at a splash for just an instant and continuing on. The sandy shoreline and point of land to the south, with the river beyond it, and, unseen, the dock. The turtles.

The camera continued its sweep away from the beach to the grass. Then the trees floated into the picture. A squirrel darted into a clearing, and the camera stopped to study it picking up something and stuffing it into its mouth. It sat on its hind legs and chewed, and the camera zoomed in on it. Behind the squirrel the trees stood thick and leafy, but a few cars were visible in the parking lot beyond. On the road an occasional car passed with a glint of sunshine and a whoosh.

And now Chris could hear a new sound, barely audible at first, and then louder but still faint, still distant. It was music—a familiar, music-box tune. He hadn't just dreamed it.

The camera stayed on the squirrel. Chris's eyes were watering. His ears were straining. He was afraid to blink. This should be the place, if his mind wasn't playing tricks on him. He waited, his mouth a dry sponge, as the music got louder and suddenly blended in with the sound of a vehicle pulling into the parking lot from the highway. Then it appeared through the trees, big and white and dappled with shade. A ghost in the shadows. And now the music was even louder, more distinctive. The vehicle, half-hidden by trees and bushes, inched across the screen and stopped, its back half still visible. For another heartbeat, Chris could hear the music. And then it stopped, replaced by the idle of a motor.

As the squirrel chewed and the engine idled, Chris watched and listened. For what seemed like an eternity, he listened. Finally, he heard a muffled thud—the sound of a car door closing—and the vehicle eased out of the picture, the rumble of its motor growing louder and then softer, as it accelerated out of the parking lot. He continued to listen until the squirrel disappeared from the screen and was replaced by blue sky and clouds. But the music didn't play again.

Chris took a deep breath and thought for a moment, his heart racing. He hit the stop button, then reverse, then stop, and then back to play. On the screen, the squirrel was eating again, quietly enjoying its food. Chris waited, listening, edging closer to the TV. When he heard the first faint strains of the music, he started counting slowly. By the time the music stopped, he'd gotten to twenty-seven. He reversed the tape, started it again, and waited. As the vehicle appeared on the screen, he hit the pause button. A still picture appeared. A picture of a squirrel and grass and trees and a large white van, frozen in the parking lot. The room was silent, as if Chris had put everything on pause. But he was conscious of his heartbeat as he slid even closer to the TV to get a better look.

Now he could see it for sure. Even out of focus and cut into sections and shaded by the trees, it was still visible. A big ice cream cone, golden yellow and chocolate brown and tilted to the right, was painted on the side of the truck. He couldn't make out the words underneath it, but he knew what they were. His heart beat faster. He could feel the pulses in his head.

He hit the pause button again, leaning his head to listen, and the tape moved forward, the music resumed. The van slowed to a stop, halfway out of the picture. The music stopped—abruptly—and Chris started counting. He got to seventy-four this time— more than a minute—before the van pulled quietly out of the picture.

The picture faded out and back in again, and several seconds of puffy white clouds in a bright blue sky filled the screen. Then it went blank. With a trembling finger he hit the stop button and then reverse, and the tape zipped backwards through the VCR. *If he was there to sell ice cream, why didn't he leave the music on?* Chris thought. *He always leaves his music on in the parking lot. And if he wasn't there to sell ice cream, why was he there?*

He counted to five, stopped the tape, and pressed the play button. The squirrel appeared again, busily chewing on its fragment of food. Chris turned up the sound. The noises he'd heard earlier were magnified, but he didn't hear anything new. He moved to within a foot of the speaker and closed his eyes, concentrating. The music started, got louder, and stopped—right in the middle of *Take Me Out to the Ball Game.*

He continued to listen, looking at the screen now, but he couldn't concentrate. The scenes changed and the screen went blank, but he sat still for a long time, staring straight ahead. What did it mean—anything? Nothing? A feeling was growing in the pit of his stomach. He didn't know if it was good or bad, but he didn't want to let it go. Missing and presumed drowned was what the radio man had said. Chris's mouth was dry and sour. He went into the kitchen, got a can of soda from the refrigerator, took a long drink, and brought it back to the family room.

The TV screen was still blank. He turned the sound down and squatted in front of it. His eyes burned from too much staring and not enough sleep. He reversed the tape, trying to think, to sort things out. He stopped it and hit the play button. Too far. His mom was just coming out of the ladies' room. Fast forward. Stop. He and Molly going into The Cloverbud. He pressed the pause button.

There it was. Parked just outside the little store, the big white van took up the whole lower right-hand corner of the screen. Chris could see the long, horn-shaped speaker on top and the painted-on ice cream cone on the side. Underneath it were the words, "The Cloverbud's Traveling Treat Truck." Farther underneath in smaller letters Chris could read, "Miles of Smiles." Little yellow smiley faces formed the dots over the i's.

For as long as Chris could remember, Clover and Bud had had the van along with their store. During the summer and on mild late spring and early fall weekends, they took turns covering a long route to the homes and beaches and parks in the Greenwater area. They sold ice cream and other frozen desserts and candy from the back of the truck. The beach park was one of their regular stops. But Chris couldn't think of a time when they'd stopped at the parking lot without the music playing the whole time. How could they sell anything if nobody knew they were there?

Maybe they could see that there weren't very many people at the beach that day. Or maybe they didn't want anyone to know they were there. But why? What would that mean? Chris didn't want to let himself even think about it.

He hit the pause button again, and he and Molly resumed their walk into The Cloverbud. The picture faded out and quickly back in, and they were coming out. Molly had her big ice cream cone in one hand. Clover was holding her other hand as they walked out together onto the sidewalk. Chris paused with Bud for a moment in the doorway, talking. What was it they were talking about? Fishing, Chris remembered. A new lure Bud had tried out. He liked to talk fishing and sports with Chris.

Chris left Bud standing in the doorway and followed Molly and Clover into the street. As they approached the car, Clover stopped and bent down to whisper something in Molly's ear. Molly smiled mischievously, nodded her head, and dashed for the car. The picture faded out. When it came back on, they were at the summer house.

Chris stopped the tape and played the Cloverbud scenes back again. He tried to think: had Molly said anything? He remembered asking her what Clover had told her. What had she answered? On the screen, Clover was whispering to her again. What was it she was saying? In desperation, he hit the single-frame advance button and the scene slowed down to a crawl. Clover's fleshy jaw and lips barely moved. Molly's smile spread across her face like an inkblot.

Chris slammed his hand into the rug in disgust. There was no way he could read Clover's lips, even at this speed, but he let the scene play on, hoping for something.

Then he remembered—a secret.

"It's a secret," Molly had said.

And he hadn't pursued it. He'd been more interested in their plans for the day than Molly's silly, little-girl secret. But so what? What if Clover had just said that she'd give her another big ice cream cone the next time she came to the store?

Chris shook his head. He was no detective. And he knew he was still having a hard time accepting that Molly was dead. But what if this feeling he was having wasn't just the brainchild of an overactive imagination, or wishful thinking, or too much spaghetti for dinner? What if Bud and Clover had something to do with her disappearance? What if she were alive somewhere now? A warm glow and a cold chill were battling it out someplace deep inside him.

He was too tired to think about it and he knew he couldn't tell anybody now. There was nothing to tell—yet. And it was very late. Or early. Predawn light was beginning to filter into the room. He stopped the tape, ejected it, and carried it up to bed with him. When he woke up, he'd need some proof that this hadn't been a dream.

**6**

CHRIS awoke with sunlight flowing through his open window and a sharp pain in his ribs. He stuck his hand between his side and the mattress and pulled out the videocassette. He *hadn't* dreamed it.

A twinge of nervous excitement rippled through his body. He looked at his clock—7:34. He hadn't gotten much sleep, but aside from a dull ache in his head, he felt good. Wide awake, he jumped from bed. He could hear his parents' voices in the kitchen. Talking, just talking to each other. He tried to remember the last time they'd done that.

He threw on some shorts and a wrinkled T-shirt and hurried downstairs. Somehow it seemed to him that he had no time to waste, although he wasn't sure what he was going to do. His mom and dad glanced up from the table in surprise when he walked into the kitchen. His dad made an exaggerated show of looking at his watch, at Chris, and back at his watch again.

"It must have stopped. What time do you have, Lynn?" he said.

His mom smiled. "Mine's stopped, too. It says seven-forty. I guess we're both late for work."

"Ha, ha," Chris said sarcastically, sitting down at the table. It wasn't the first time he'd gotten up this early during the summer. He could think of at least one other time.

"What's the occasion?" his dad asked.

Chris thought for a moment, pretending to study the side of a cereal box. "Nothing," he said finally. "I just figured I better get used to getting up earlier. School's starting in two weeks." He poured himself some cereal and milk and spooned it into his mouth. He'd swallowed three mouthfuls before he realized that he didn't even know what kind of cereal it was. His mind was racing, cutting off everything else in the room.

"What did you think about the tape last night, Chris?" his mom asked. The question startled him, bringing him back. He looked at his mom's face, but he could feel his dad's eyes on him. He chewed his cereal a long time before swallowing.

"The tape?" *Now that was a bright reply.* "I, uh,

thought it was fine. I mean, it was nice seeing Molly. Nice to be reminded of how she was. Not as painful as I thought." He considered for a moment, wondering if they'd like to know what he really thought, then resumed reading the cereal box.

"That's what we felt, too," his mom said. "We're really glad we have the tape. Thanks for helping us take it, Chris."

"It weren't nothin'," he said. "I think dad shot most of the good scenes, anyway. I especially enjoyed the classic restroom exit."

His dad laughed. His mom shook her head. "I think I've seen that scene too many times," she said. "Originality is not one of your father's strong points."

Chris took another bite of cereal and stared out the window at the basketball hoop and pine trees in the backyard. He turned a question over in his mind until he thought it sounded okay. "Mom," he finally said. She looked up from some work papers she'd been studying. "Do you remember on the day we lost Molly, when you ran to the phone to call the police and firemen?"

His mom stared at him and nodded her head slowly. She set her cup down on an angle, spilling coffee on the white table top. His dad looked quizzically across the table at him. "Yes, I do, Chris," she said. "I won't ever forget it."

"When you got to the phone," he continued, "did

you see anything in the parking lot? Anything unusual, I mean?"

"Like what?" she said, twisting her wedding ring around on her finger.

"Was Clover and Bud's ice cream truck there?"

She looked at him blankly.

"Did you see it?" he said. "Do you remember hearing it?"

She continued to look in his direction, but he could see her focusing on another scene, far away in miles and time.

"No," she said. "Just cars. Just a few cars in the parking lot. If I had seen Clover or Bud there, I would have asked them for help. I'm sure they weren't. And I don't remember hearing the music."

"Neither do I, Chris," his dad said. "But why are you asking?"

Chris had his answer ready. "Oh, I was doing what Dr. Wilde said. You know, trying to visualize what happened that day. Remembering everything and dealing with it now, instead of putting off dealing with it."

His dad searched Chris's face, looking for the real explanation there, no doubt. But Chris maintained his best sincere expression.

Finally his dad smiled. A bit forced, but he smiled. "Seems like a good idea," he said. He got up from the table and carried his dishes to the sink. His thoughts seemed to be somewhere else.

"Do you think they'll ever find her? Her body, I mean?" Chris asked. He wasn't convinced that some-one—even a small someone—could drown and never be found. He wanted his parents to tell him that everyone who had ever drowned in the river had been recovered. He watched his dad turn and look at his mom. His dad looked as if he wanted to avoid answering this one. She glanced up from her work papers at his dad, and then at Chris. Her face had suddenly turned gray. Chris was sorry he'd asked the question. He wanted to yell, "But what if she isn't even dead? Maybe she's alive!" Instead he said, "I mean, does it really happen that someone could drown in a river and never be found?"

"It happens, Chris," his dad finally said. "Molly drowned in a big river. It's possible that her body won't ever be found."

"Oh," Chris said. But that didn't prove anything to him, just that she *could* have drowned. It didn't mean she *had*. It didn't mean there wasn't a real reason why his heart was thumping like a large rabbit in his chest. It didn't mean he couldn't try to find out what that reason was.

"But we hope they do find her sometime soon," his mom said, her eyes glistening in the sunlight filtering through the kitchen curtains. "We'd all feel better if she were closer to us, if we knew where she was. I know *I* would."

"Me, too, Mom," Chris said. "Me, too."

His dad walked over to the table, gave them each a hug, and went upstairs to finish getting ready for work.

Chris's heart was beating loudly. He was afraid his mom would be able to hear it from across the table. "Is it okay if Pat and I ride our bikes over to the mall today, Mom? We thought we'd look around for school clothes and go to a movie. And then I'm invited to his house for dinner."

"That sounds fine, Chris. It looks as if I may have to work late tonight, anyway. Do you need money for the show?"

"No, I've got enough."

"Well, if you find any clothes you like, we can go back and look at them tomorrow night," she said.

"Okay, Mom." He jumped up from the table and sprinted upstairs to the phone in his room. After calling the bus depot, he dialed Pat's number. He asked Pat's mom to get him out of bed.

Pat dropped his phone once before picking it up and managing a sleepy grunt. Chris waited until he heard Pat's mom hang up the other phone. "Are you by yourself?" he asked.

"Yeah. What time is it, anyway?" Pat mumbled.

"It's getting late. We've only got an hour to get to the bus depot."

"Excuse my ignorance, but why do we want to go to the bus depot?" Pat was waking up.

"We need to catch the 9:00 bus to Greenwater."

"You just got back from Greenwater."

"Brilliant, Pat. But you're wasting a lot of time. I need to go back there. Can you go with me? I'll explain it all to you on the way."

"I'll ask my mom, but I don't think she'll go for it."

"Mine wouldn't have either. She thinks we're riding our bikes to the mall to look for clothes, seeing a movie, and going back to your house for dinner. You better give yours the same story. Except make it dinner at my house."

Pat was silent for a moment. "What time are we coming back?" he said finally.

"I don't know. It depends on what we find. Before dark, anyway. The buses run every two hours."

More silence on the other end. Then, "Chris?"

"Yeah?" Chris could feel his patience disappearing and his stress level going up.

"What are we going there for?"

"I'll tell you later. Just go ask your mom." He heard the phone clunk down on Pat's table, then silence. He waited, nervously glancing at his watch. *Say it's okay*, he thought, concentrating hard.

Then Pat was back. "My mom says yes, Mystery Man. I can be ready in ten minutes. How much money do I need?"

Chris allowed himself a sigh of relief. He didn't want to make this trip alone. "The bus is eighteen dollars round trip. And we'll need some money for food—I'd say another five bucks or so. Do you need some money?"

"I've got some saved. I'll let you buy me some ice cream at The Cloverbud, though."

Chris shook off a chill. "I'll do that," he said. Suddenly he pictured Clover and Bud standing behind the counter, smiling down at Molly. "I'll be there in ten minutes. Then I figure it's fifteen minutes to the bus depot on our bikes. That should give us enough time to get the tickets and catch the nine o'clock bus."

"Sounds good," Pat said. "But I have to admit you've got me real curious. I hope you have a good story for me."

"I'll let you decide," Chris said and hung up.

**7**

**THE** big silver bus pulled out of the Milwaukee depot at 9:05. Chris and Pat sat near the back, surrounded by empty seats. The only other passengers—a thin scarecrow of a woman with four noisy, scruffy little kids and an old man with an unlit, half-smoked cigar in his mouth—were seated near the front. They hadn't gone six blocks before the old man got up and moved toward the back, taking a seat three rows in front of the boys. Chris watched him turn down his hearing aid.

"You think the bikes will be okay?" Pat asked.

"I think so. They're chained to the pole and the pole's holding up the building. I don't think anyone's going to move it—not without a cutting torch, or dynamite."

"I hope you're right. You got any food?"

Chris shook his head. "I didn't have time to grab any. We can get something when we get there." His mind drifted away; he thought about what they would do when they got there. What was the first step going to be? Should he walk right in and ask Bud and Clover to give back his little sister? And have them laugh at him? Or feel sorry for him? Or get angry? Or if they really had her, decide that they were in danger and needed to do something desperate?

No, walking in and accusing them of anything would be stupid. He'd have to think of something else, some other way to find out if there was really something to this dream he was having. Maybe their faces would give them away. Maybe he could just look in their eyes and know for sure. And then what?

He was staring out the window, but he could feel Pat's eyes on him. He turned toward his friend. It was time to let him in on it.

"You going to tell me what we're doing, Christopher?" Pat asked.

Chris nodded his head. "Yeah. But you've got to let me get through the whole story before you start laughing or calling me crazy. Okay?"

"Okay."

Chris began slowly, trying to remember how he first got the feeling that something wasn't making sense to him. He told Pat about the uneasiness he'd gone to bed with after seeing the tape. How he'd woken up twice, the second time recalling a scene and sounds on the tape that didn't seem to fit. What he'd seen and heard when he watched the tape again. The earlier scene in town. And Molly's secret.

He tried not to make anything sound more significant than it was, but as the words came out he could feel the excitement building. Pat listened quietly. Chris couldn't tell what he was thinking. When Chris stopped talking Pat just sat there, staring at the back of the seat in front of him. He wasn't laughing.

Chris waited for a response. It wasn't like Pat to be quiet for more than a minute at a time. Chris just needed him to say something halfway positive, like maybe there was something to it.

"It's possible," he said finally. "I think it really is possible." He frowned deeply. "But maybe it's nothing. There isn't much to go on; it could be just coincidence."

"I know," Chris said, but he felt as if a weight had been lifted. Pat didn't think he was crazy.

"Why haven't you told your parents?" Pat asked.

"Because I didn't think I had enough to tell them. I figured they'd think I was fooling myself, or they'd get their hopes up over nothing. Or they'd just plain get upset. I wanted to see if I could find out anything on my own."

"On *our* own, you mean."

"Yeah. I was hoping you could come; I may need a bodyguard, or at least a friend."

"You going to be disappointed if this doesn't get us anywhere?"

"What do *you* think? But there's nothing I can do about that."

Pat sat back in his seat and let out a sigh. "But wouldn't it be something if she *were*, Chris—still alive, I mean?" he said.

"Yeah," Chris said. "It would."

"So what do we do when we get there?"

"I haven't come up with a definite plan. Just play it by ear and be careful. Pretend we're detectives without looking like we are. Clover and Bud live in an apartment attached to the back of their shop. I've seen it from the alley. If they've got Molly, she'd have to be there."

8

**THE** bus made one quick stop at the Greenwater Drug Store before proceeding through the little town. Chris and Pat were left standing on the sunny sidewalk in a swirl of dust and exhaust fumes. From a block away, The Cloverbud reached out to them like a magnet. Chris could feel its presence, and he knew Pat felt it, too. Without speaking, they started across the street.

Chris felt conspicuous, even though he'd walked this same street dozens of times before. This time, it was different. This time, he wasn't supposed to be here, and he had a feeling that it showed on his face.

Pat grabbed Chris's arm and pointed in the direction of The Cloverbud. "The van's not there, Chris," he said. "Isn't that kind of weird?"

"Why?" Chris said.

"It's a little early in the day for ice cream, isn't it?"

"I guess you're right," Chris said. But he could think of some other places the van could be—the alley behind the shop, for instance.

They approached Cowbutter Cookies. The smells of fresh baking drifted down the sidewalk and filled Chris's nose. He and Pat glanced quickly at each other, silently agreeing that the cookies smelled great. But they walked right past the open door and its tempting smells, right past the bookstore with its shiny book covers and posters displayed in the window, and stopped abruptly at the door to The Cloverbud.

Chris's stomach tightened up. It was closed. The same CLOSED sign that had been hanging in the window two days ago was still there. And it was hanging at the same odd angle. He looked at Pat, who was frowning and peering into the dark store.

"Come here and look at this, Chris," Pat said.

Chris walked up to the big window and stared through cupped hands into the shadowy interior. The knot in his stomach got tighter. Everything was gone: all the jars and boxes and equipment, all the tables and chairs and stuff on the walls—gone. The only things left were the big freezer display case and counter where the ice cream was kept, and some built-in cabinets.

"Have they left for the winter already?" Pat asked.

"Not this early. Never this early—it's still August. They always stay past Labor Day—usually till October." Chris turned and looked at Pat. *What next?* he thought. The sun was hot on the back of his neck, but he felt cold.

"Why don't we try next door?" Pat said. "Maybe they can tell us something."

The sales clerk in the bookstore was a high school girl who didn't know much about her neighbors.

"I only saw them a few times after I started work here," she told Chris.

Something about her words didn't sound right, didn't sound like what he'd expected to hear. "When did you start?" Chris asked. He felt weighted down suddenly, but he smiled, trying to keep the conversation light, trying to keep her talking.

She thought for a moment. "I don't remember, exactly," she said, "but it was a few weeks before school got out—around the middle of May, I guess."

"So when was the last time you saw them?" Pat said. His question was offhand, casual-sounding, but Chris could tell by the pitch of his voice that he was on edge—that he wanted an answer.

The girl hesitated for a moment, looking half-annoyed, but then she glanced at Pat's face and decided to continue. Her only real customers—a young couple going through a table of books in the far corner of the store—weren't ready to be waited on, anyway. "A week," she said, finally. "About a week."

"You saw them a week ago?" Pat said.

"No, a week after I *started*," she said. "The last time I saw them—her, at least—was maybe a week after I came to work. He—Bud—was around here a while after that—probably another couple of weeks or so."

Chris felt suffocated now, as if somebody were sitting on his chest. He took a deep breath and let it out slowly. "And you haven't seen them since?" he said.

"No," she said, shaking her head. "Are they friends of yours?"

"They were," Chris said. "We were hoping to see them again." He was still hoping to see them again— now, more than ever.

"The Cloverbud's been closed since June?" Pat said.

"Closed tight," she said. "And there's nowhere else to get ice cream around here."

"Where'd they go?" Pat asked. His casual tone was gone.

"I don't know," she said.

"Who does?" Chris asked.

"I don't know that, either," she said. "But somebody should."

Chris was about out of questions—except one. "Does anybody know why they left?" he asked. "Right at the beginning of summer, I mean?"

She shrugged her shoulders. "Sorry," she said.

"That's okay," Chris said, starting for the door.

"Thanks," Pat said.

"Sure," she said. "Hope you find them."

Chris and Pat drifted back outside. The smell of fresh cookies still hung in the air.

"They were gone by the middle of June," Pat said.

"That's what I figured, too," Chris said. But why? And where? "Let's go into Cowbutter," he said.

"I'm not really hungry," Pat said, looking agitated.

Chris knew the feeling. He was having a hard time keeping his own emotions under control. "Me, neither, Pat. But if anybody knows anything about what's going on, Helen and Frank will. She even writes a column for the newspaper."

But it was Helen's husband, Frank, who would give them their next bit of news. Just as short and blocky as Helen, he stood behind the counter smiling at them as they walked into the little store. "Chris!" he bellowed, his voice filling the room. "Helen told me you were in Saturday. Nice to see you." He looked at Pat. "And I see you brought your bodyguard. When are you going to quit growing, Pat?"

"Not for a while, I hope. There aren't many small guys playing college football."

"I wouldn't worry about it," Frank said. "You're already out of the *small* category." He looked back at

Chris. "What can I do for you guys?" he said.

"How about a half dozen assorted," Chris said, laying a five-dollar bill on the counter. Maybe they'd be hungry later. "Can you tell me something?"

"I'll try, Chris. As long as it's not a weather forecast or a prediction on how the Packers are going to do this year."

"Nothing that tough. At least I don't think so. I'm just wondering if you know when Bud and Clover are getting back."

Frank looked at Chris curiously.

"I, uh, borrowed a fishing book from him a while back and I just want to return it," Chris said quickly. He wondered how truthful that sounded. He didn't think he was a very good liar.

"They're not getting back," Frank said. "Not this year, anyway. They had to leave early. Real early. Sometime in June, I think it was. Clover was gone even before that—before Memorial Day, I recall."

"Why?" Pat asked.

"Clover's mom took sick, I guess. Couldn't manage on her own, anymore."

"They couldn't bring her up here?" Pat said.

"Guess not. They didn't say much about it."

Chris could feel sweat trickling down his back. What did all this mean? Should he be glad they'd left town? Did it mean they'd gotten nervous about something? Or was Clover's mom really sick? Just how far should he let his imagination prowl?

"Do you know where they went—where Clover's mom lives?" Chris asked.

Frank thought while he put some cookies in a bag and placed Chris's change on the counter. "Not really, Chris. Come to think of it, they never said exactly. Down south somewhere. Someplace warmer, I know. I got the feeling it was a small town like this. A resort area or a place with vacation homes. They run the same kind of business down there in the winter. You know, an ice cream store and the truck and everything."

Chris ran his hand through his hair. This wasn't getting any easier. What to do next? There still wasn't anything to go on. "So how can I get their mailing address to send Bud the book?" he asked.

"I don't know. The post office might have it, but I'm not sure they'd give it to you. Or Carol Sweeney over at the real estate office might help. She handles the leases for this building."

"Leases?" Pat said.

"Yeah," Frank said. "We—all the businesses here—lease our spaces. A lease is kind of like a rental agreement. When you fill one out, you have to give the realtor a lot of information about yourself."

Chris thought for a moment. He wasn't sure if this was good news or bad, but it did explain how Bud and Clover got out of town so fast: they didn't own their store. "The apartment in back—where they lived—was leased, too?" he said.

"All of it," Frank said. "A package deal."

"You think they'll be back in the spring?" Pat asked.

"You boys have your curiosity up today, don't you?" Frank said. He shook his head thoughtfully. "But I really don't know. Neither of them talked much before they left. We thought maybe they were having family problems, but they didn't say anything to us about it. To tell you the truth, Helen made quite an effort to find out what was going on, and even *she* couldn't come up with anything. Other than Clover's mom wasn't feeling well, that is."

Chris looked at Pat and saw something in his eyes that gave him some encouragement, that backed up the feeling he was having that something wasn't right. He picked up the bag of cookies and his change and started for the door.

"Thanks," he said. He stopped just inside the doorway and turned back. "One other thing."

"Sure. I'm not exactly busy here this morning."

Chris knew what he wanted to say, but couldn't get it out. "The day Molly disappeared—" he managed, finally, and then stopped, searching for the right words. "The day we lost Molly—thanks for helping look for her." He couldn't say the word *drowned*—not now, he couldn't.

"It was nothing, Chris."

Chris opened his mouth to say something but was stopped by Frank's upraised hand.

"I mean it," Frank said. "I felt completely worthless out there that day. I would've done anything to really help." Visibly upset, he slammed the cash register door closed.

"Did you see Bud or Clover there?" Chris asked quickly. Now Frank looked confused. "I mean, were they helping, too?"

Frank thought for a long moment, staring at the floor, scratching the bald spot on the crown of his head. When he looked up, there was a question—not an answer—in his eyes.

"Chris's counselor thinks it's a good idea to have all this stuff clear in his mind," Pat said quickly.

"Oh? I suppose it is," Frank said distractedly, rubbing his chin and staring off into space.

Chris waited for him to go on.

"They weren't there," Frank said finally. "I remember now, as soon as we heard about the trouble, I went over to get them because I knew they'd want to help. But the truck was gone, and the place was closed up. They had a CLOSED sign on the door. Must have both been out making their rounds in the truck. Or maybe one of them was in the truck and one was somewhere else. It was a slow day, as I remember it. And I don't recall seeing them anywhere else. It was late when I got back here."

"Right," Chris said. "Thanks again."

"You bet. Hope it helps. We're real sorry about your little sister."

"Thanks," Chris said. He hurried from the store, took a quick left, and headed down the sidewalk, breaking into a jog.

"Where to?" Pat asked, falling in step next to him.

"The post office. Maybe they'll tell us something."

But Mr. Armstrong at the post office couldn't help. "They asked us to stop delivery as of June fourteenth," he said, checking his records, "and left no forwarding address."

"Isn't that unusual?" Chris asked him. He was feeling frustrated, but also more and more as if there really was a reason for his suspicions. And part of him was relieved that Clover and Bud were gone. What if he'd already found them and there was no Molly? His search and all his hope would be finished.

"I guess it is odd," Mr. Armstrong said, "but it happens. Sometimes people don't particularly want their junk mail following them across the country."

The boys walked back outside into the bright sunlight. Pat offered Chris the bag of cookies. He took one, biting into it absentmindedly.

"What do you think, Pat?" Chris asked.

"I think we better go to the real estate office," Pat said.

Chris nodded and they started walking down the sidewalk again.

"I also think there may be nothing to this, but things smell a lot fishier now than when we left home this morning. Bud and Clover are acting like they've got something to hide," Pat said.

"Or some*one*," Chris said. Not so easy to say, but it was what he was hoping for, what he was praying for: that she wasn't at the bottom of the river. That Bud and Clover had taken her. That she was still alive. "But why? Why would they do it?" he asked Pat.

"Who knows?" Pat said. "But I've heard of it happening. It could have happened to Molly. Let's hope so."

They came to the end of the block and crossed the street to the real estate office. Carol Sweeney was sitting at a cluttered desk, looking through a thick book and making notes on a yellow tablet, when they walked in.

She looked up at them and smiled, her blue eyes twinkling behind thick glasses. Carol had sold Chris's mom and dad their summer house many years before. "Hi, Chris. Hi, Pat. How are you guys doing?" she asked. "I didn't realize you were in the market for some real estate."

"Hi," Chris said.

"Hi, Mrs. Sweeney," Pat said.

*His polite young man routine,* Chris thought. Well, maybe it would help. But how was Chris going to ask for the information he wanted? Pat gave him a little time to think about it.

"Yeah, we're looking for some property, Mrs. Sweeney," Pat said. "You know, something in keeping with our social status. An acre of waterfront, say, with a six-bedroom house, fireplaces, hot tub, pool, and a ski boat and float plane moored to the dock. You got anything like that?"

"I might," Carol said with a straight face. "How much money do you have?"

Pat turned his front pockets inside out and came up with a handful of change. "Looks like about ninety-three cents."

"I don't think that will quite do it," Carol said.

"How about if I throw in a cookie?" Pat said, holding the bag out to her.

"It's a deal," she said, digging through the bag and pulling out a chocolate chip cookie dipped in chocolate. "I can't resist these things."

Chris decided that he'd come right to the point. Sort of. "Carol, do you know anything about Clover and Bud?" he said. "Where they went, I mean, and whether they're coming back or not?"

"Those are good questions, Chris," she said, studying his face. "But I'm afraid I don't know the answers. This year's an option year on their lease, which means they have until the end of August to let us know if they're going to renew. I haven't heard anything yet. As far as where they went, I don't have any idea. I barely talked to them before they left."

Chris's disappointment must have shown. "Did they owe you some money or something, Chris?" Carol asked.

Chris felt his face grow warm. "No, uh, I...I think maybe Molly left her bear in The Cloverbud the last time we were there. I'd like to get it back for my folks to have." He might as well try out a new story.

"Oh. That's too bad," she said, sounding as if she meant it. "I've been through the place a couple of times since they left, though, and there's nothing there. You've probably seen how empty the shop is, if you looked through the window. The apartment's the same—completely vacant. There's no place for a bear—or even a toy mouse—to hide. Maybe Molly left it somewhere else. Or Clover and Bud didn't know whose it was and gave it away."

"Or threw it away," Pat said. "Do you think they'd have anything left in their garbage can?"

Chris looked at him, wondering where he was going with this.

"After—what's it been—two months?" Carol said. "I doubt it, but it's possible, I guess. They have a small dumpster in the alley, if you want to take a look."

"Nobody would care?" Pat said.

"Not unless there's some really valuable garbage in there."

"We might as well, then, huh, Chris?"

Chris glanced at him again. Did the poor guy think there really was a bear? "Sure," he said. "It's worth a look."

9

**"THERE'S** no bear," Chris said, once they were out on the sidewalk and headed up the block.

"What?" Pat said.

"I made up the bear story," Chris said.

"I knew that," Pat said. "I never saw Molly with a bear."

"You knew it?"

"Yeah. I just played along because I thought it would give us an excuse to snoop around over there, in case someone wonders what we're doing."

"You think we'll really find anything?" Chris asked. "In the garbage, I mean?"

"Who knows?" Pat said. "But where else do we have to look?"

Chris thought for a minute while they crossed the

street, heading away from The Cloverbud to the next block, where they'd go left and then left again into the alley, doubling back toward the apartment. It was the only way to get there without going through the store. "I guess we *don't* have any other choices right now," he said. He couldn't think of anything, at least.

"Maybe we'll come up with some more ideas while we're looking," Pat said.

"Yeah," Chris said. But except for giving them a chance to think, he figured this was going to be a waste of time. He couldn't imagine the dumpster being anything but empty. If Bud and Clover really *were* trying to hide their trail, they'd done a good job of it so far; Chris didn't expect that to change.

As they hurried down the dusty alley, looking for the back of The Cloverbud, his mind kept working, not letting up. There had to be some other ways to find out where Bud and Clover went—some ways he and Pat just hadn't thought of yet, or maybe didn't even know about. They couldn't have run into a road-block, already—not this soon.

But what if they had? Or were about to? What if there was nothing at the apartment, and they couldn't think of anywhere else to turn? Then what? Should he tell his parents? The police? Maybe the police could track them down. But why would they want to? He still had no proof of anything—not even any concrete reasons to be suspicious. But he was more than suspicious. Despite some doubts, he had a feeling—a deep-down feeling—that Molly wasn't in that river, that Bud and Clover had taken her, and that their reason for leaving town so quickly and quietly had nothing to do with Clover's mom being sick. Chris just had to figure out how to get back on the track.

"Any ideas, Pat?" he said.

"Not really," Pat said. "Everything's going nowhere. I was just trying to think if there was some way to find out if Clover's mom really is sick. But then we'd have to find out where she lives—if she's even alive—and if we knew that, we'd know where Bud and Clover are, too."

"Which we don't."

"Right."

"So that idea won't work."

"That's what I meant," Pat said. "Everything's going nowhere. Or at least back to us needing to find out where they went."

Chris glanced to his left and saw a familiar name—The Cloverbud—painted in white letters on one of the mailboxes attached to the building. Next to it was the door that must have been the entrance to the apartment—the back entrance to the store. On one side of the entrance was a small shrub, brown and dry and dead from neglect. On the other side, a battered dumpster squatted, the lid closed.

They stopped, glanced at each other, and then headed across the small, weedy yard. *Here goes nothing*, Chris thought.

They reached the dumpster and stood there, frozen.

"Be my guest," Pat said finally, pointing to the lid.

Chris opened it slowly, afraid to look down, to look inside, but he heard Pat mutter something under his breath, and he knew he didn't have to look. When at last he did, he wasn't surprised—just disappointed. It was empty—as empty as he felt right now. "Not even a gum wrapper," he said.

"Sorry," Pat said. "It was a waste of time."

"It didn't take much time," Chris said. "And we need to check out everything we can think of."

"Yeah," Pat said, "but I can't think of anything else. What do we do now?"

"I don't know," Chris said. "Looks like we've hit a dead end. I think we're going to have to talk to somebody about getting the police in on this. They know how to track people down."

"You going to tell your dad?"

"I guess I'll have to. Then he can talk to the police. I just don't know if anyone will believe me."

"Us," Pat said. "I'll back you up on this."

Chris looked at his watch. "We've got over an hour till the next bus gets here. Maybe if we grab something to eat, and wander around a while, we'll come up with something."

He looked at Pat, waiting for an answer. "Okay, Pat?" he said. But Pat was looking right past him, right past his ear. "Pat?"

"That their mailbox, Chris?" Pat said.

Chris turned and saw what Pat was staring at. "Looks like it to me," he said.

"I think there's something in it."

Chris looked closer. Through slits in the brown metal he could see white paper. He glanced over his shoulder to see if anyone was watching, but the alley was vacant in both directions. When he turned back, Pat was already lifting the small lid and removing the contents of the box.

"What do we have here?" Pat said.

Chris shouldered in next to him, eyeing the small stack of mail in Pat's hand.

The top piece was a white window envelope addressed to Mr. Bud Butler at 146 Date Street, Greenwater. The envelope was from Larson Dairy Products in Crescent, a larger town about ten miles away. Maybe a bill, Chris decided.

"Junk," Pat said, and moved it to the bottom of the pile.

The next piece was a coupon envelope addressed to "Resident." Then another white envelope, this one from an insurance agency in Crescent, addressed to Mr. and Mrs. Leon Butler.

"Leon?" Pat said.

"His real name," Chris said. "You think his parents named him Bud?"

"You never know," Pat said.

A postcard advertising a magazine was next. Pat quickly shuffled it to the bottom of the pile.

Another white envelope followed. But this one was different. Chris stared at it, trying to figure out what it was doing in Bud and Clover's mailbox.

"What's this?" Pat said.

But Chris didn't answer. He was listening to his heart accelerating inside his chest. The envelope wasn't addressed to Bud and Clover. It wasn't addressed to anyone in Greenwater, or Crescent. It was addressed to a Barnlow Realty in someplace called New Moon Bay. In Florida. And stamped next to the address were the words ATTEMPTED, NOT KNOWN. Above that stamp was another one—a hand, pointing a finger toward the upper left hand corner of the envelope, where the return address was neatly written. RETURNED TO SENDER was printed on the hand, and below that, the words ADDRESSEE UNKNOWN.

The post office had gotten its message across: they couldn't deliver the mail, so they'd returned it to the return address—146 Date Street, Greenwater. The envelope hadn't been sent *to* Clover and Bud; it had been sent *from* them.

"The post office sent it back, didn't it," Pat said.

"That's what it looks like." Chris heard his voice quavering.

"But I thought they'd stopped their mail delivery," Pat said. "How did these get in the box?"

"I don't know," Chris said, not really caring. The important thing was that they *were* in the box. But Pat shuffled through the mail, and Chris noticed something. "They're all postmarked between June ninth and twelfth," Chris said.

"Except for this one," Pat said, holding up the returned envelope and handing it to Chris. "June 6th," he said.

"I think they postmark the mail where you send it from," Chris said, examining the envelope. "It needed time to get down and back. But it looks like they all got delivered before June fourteenth—the day Mr. Armstrong said they'd stopped delivering. Probably only a day or two before."

"Maybe Bud forgot to check his mail right before he left," Pat said.

"That's what I was thinking," Chris said. "Or maybe he left town a little earlier than he'd planned."

They stood—silent—in the shadow of the building. A soft whisper of a breeze pushed past Chris's face. Suddenly the air smelled sweeter.

"Florida," Pat said. "That's definitely south."

"Do you think there's an ice cream store in New

Moon Bay?" Chris said. He couldn't help smiling.

"I think we better find out," Pat said, meeting Chris's smile with one of his own.

They hurried to the phone booth in front of the gas station, where they pulled all the change from their pockets and set it on the shelf under the phone.

"What's it cost to call Florida?" Chris asked.

"In the middle of the day?" Pat said. "Probably a lot."

"We've got $1.53," Chris said, pushing the last of the coins into a small pile.

"Not enough," Pat said. "At least I don't think so. We'll have to go in and get some change." He started to pull out his wallet, but Chris stopped him.

"Wait!" Chris said. "I just remembered: I've got my parents' credit card number for long distance calls."

"They gave you their credit card number?" Pat said in disbelief.

"For emergencies," Chris said. "I've never used it before." He pulled a small slip of paper from a corner of his wallet and unfolded it. A number was written on it in his mom's handwriting. All he had to do was punch it in at the end of his area code and phone number, and he was in business. He wondered how she'd feel if she knew what he was about to use it for—how his mom and dad would feel about everything he was up to today. He had an idea that they wouldn't trust him quite as much anymore. But this was something he had to do.

"My parents gave me something for emergencies, too," Pat said. "Some advice. They said to always carry a quarter with me." He had the phone book open, looking through the area code directory in the front. He found Florida, and ran his finger down the list of codes. "There's four area codes for Florida," he said. "Call information for all of 'em."

When Chris finally dialed, he felt as if he were punching enough numbers to call Mars. It worked, though, and he got the right area code for New Moon Bay on his second try. But the operator had no listing for a Bud or Clover or even a Leon Butler. He hung up, looked at Pat, and shook his head. "Nothing," he said.

"What next?" Pat asked.

"I don't know. Maybe they don't live right in New Moon Bay, but I don't know the names of any other towns around there. Maybe we can get a map of Florida."

Chris was about to suggest that they head for the town's little library to take a look at a United States atlas when he had another idea. "You think they call their store The Cloverbud down there?" he asked.

Pat smiled. "Could be," he said. "It would probably make things easier for them."

Chris punched in Florida information again. His head was pounding. "Do you have a listing for an ice cream store called The Cloverbud in New Moon Bay?" he asked the operator.

"Checking," she said in his ear. After what seemed like a year she said, "I show no listing for The Cloverbud."

He asked her to try Clover and Bud's, and Bud and Clover's, and Butler's. Still nothing—and he'd run out of ideas. He hung up the phone again and looked at his watch. A half hour until the next bus now. Should they just get something to eat, get on the bus, and go home? Maybe they'd come up with some ideas on the way. Or maybe they wouldn't. Maybe he'd just have to try to convince his parents that they needed to get the police involved. But what were the chances of that? He was certain that he and Pat hadn't come up with enough to interest the police; he wasn't even confident that his mom and dad would take the evidence—if you could call it that—seriously.

He wiped his sweaty hands on his T-shirt. Something crinkled under the pressure, stiff against his skin. The envelope. He'd stuck it inside his shirt when they'd left Bud and Clover's house. He pulled it out, holding it up to Pat. "I think we need to look in here, don't you?"

"It's probably against the law," Pat said, grabbing the envelope and tearing it open. He removed a piece of note paper. Another piece of paper fluttered to the pavement. Chris picked it up. It was a drawing—a rough sketch of a room.

"Dear Mr. Barnlow," Pat read aloud, holding the note in front of him.

> The estimate you forwarded to me from Pelican Construction seems to be a fair one. You should have the signed lease by now, so please see to it that the remodeling gets started as soon as possible. We have already talked about what I need to have done to the space, but I am enclosing a drawing of what I have in mind, in case there is any confusion. Please share it with the construction people, and when you're in Westview, I'd appreciate your checking on their progress. We'd like to be up and running by the end of the summer. Thanks.
>
> Bud and Clover Butler.

Pat lifted his eyes to Chris. Even in the bright sunshine, they seemed to be on fire. "You think Westview is another town near New Moon Bay?" Pat asked.

"Could be," Chris replied. "Bud was expecting this Barnlow guy to be going there, according to the note." He turned back to the phone. "Let's give it another try."

His fingers were trembling as he pushed the buttons for information again. The operator answered.

"I'd like information for Westview, please," Chris said.

"Go ahead," she said.

"I need two numbers. One for a Leon, Bud, or Clover Butler. The other one would be for The Cloverbud. It's an ice cream store."

"Thank you," she said. After a long pause she was back. "Checking under Butler and The Cloverbud I find nothing in Westview," she said.

"Oh." Chris's heart sank. He looked over at Pat, who was holding the envelope and a broken pencil hopefully, waiting for a number. Chris shook his head at him. "Thanks—" he began into the phone, when the operator interrupted him.

"Could it be a new listing, hon?" she asked.

A new listing. Chris hadn't thought about it being a new listing.

"Could be," Chris said. "Yeah. It could be a new listing."

"Checking," she said.

"I have both, hon," she said a moment later.

*Both*? Chris thought. *Both numbers*? Now tears were coming to his eyes. "Can I have them please?" he asked. He looked at Pat, who was jumping up and down and waving the envelope and pencil in the air, a silly grin on his face. Chris's heart was beating so loudly that he was afraid he wouldn't be able to hear the operator.

"Sure thing," she replied. "The new listing for Leon Butler is 546-1368. For The Cloverbud Ice Cream and Confectionery Shop it's 546-1224."

"That's 546-1368 for Leon Butler and 546-1224 for The Cloverbud," Chris said loudly. Pat was writing furiously.

"That's right, hon. You gonna have a better day now?"

A better day? Chris hadn't realized his disappointment had been so obvious. "It just got better," he said. "A lot better. Thanks for all your help."

"You bet, hon," she said, and disconnected.

Still smiling, Pat handed the envelope to Chris. "Go for it," he said.

"Call them? Now?"

"Just hang up if you get an answer."

Chris punched in The Cloverbud's number and the credit card number and waited. He hung up on the tenth ring. "No one's at the store," he said.

"It's not the end of the summer yet. Maybe it isn't even open."

"Could be," Chris said, "especially since this letter never got there." He was pushing Bud and Clover's home number now. He hit the credit card numbers, heard the recorded voice say, "Thank you," and waited. The phone rang. Once. Twice. Three times. Four times. Then a sleepy voice was saying, "Hello."

*Clover's voice.*

Chris was having a hard time breathing. He was afraid he was going to make some kind of noise into the phone. But he couldn't hang up. He wanted to scream at her, to warn her that she better be nice to his baby sister because he was on his way. To tell her that everything would be forgiven if she would just give Molly back. He wanted to pretend he was a little kid and ask if Molly could come to the phone.

But he said nothing. He looked at Pat and nodded, and Pat's face brightened.

"Hello?" Clover said again, more awake now, sounding even more like herself. He imagined her saying, "Hello, Chris," back at The Cloverbud just a few months ago. It was the same voice.

He hung up softly. "It was Clover," he told Pat.

"Really?"

"I'm sure of it." He was trying to stay calm, but he felt as if his feet were floating off the ground.

In a split second they were. Pat had gotten him into a bear hug and lifted him a foot off the pavement, dancing around in a circle and laughing.

"Put me down, King Kong," Chris chuckled, and squirmed out of Pat's grasp. "We haven't exactly proven anything, you know."

"Yeah, but we're moving again. We're not at a dead end anymore. We actually know where they are."

*They.* Chris liked the sound of the word *they.* When he heard it, he thought about Clover and Bud, but mostly he thought about Molly. "Thanks to a letter that ended up where it started," he said.

"What now?" Pat asked.

Chris glanced at his watch. "We've got ten minutes till the bus gets here."

"That gives us five minutes to grab a hot dog at Fast Freddy's," Pat said, taking off down the street toward the little drive-in restaurant and the bus stop beyond. "Let's go!"

**CHRIS** sat in the family room on the edge of a chair, listening to the murmur of his parents' voices floating in from the kitchen. The television was on, but he wasn't watching it. He alternated between looking at the wall clock and through the window at the front yard, where tree shadows were stretching in the setting sun. It was 7:45; Pat was due at 8:00.

He and Pat had agreed on the bus ride home that—on paper, at least—their evidence wasn't exactly overwhelming. But now that they knew where Bud and Clover were, they didn't have a choice; they *needed* to get some help. The next step had to be to get Chris's parents involved. Chris and Pat figured that together they'd be able to convince Chris's folks that Molly had been kidnapped, or at least that there was a chance she had.

Chris had the videotape loaded and forwarded to the scene at The Cloverbud. All he needed to do was hit the "play" button, point out what had got him started, and tell them the rest of the story. The envelope sat next to him on the end table. He glanced over at it. Along with the tape, it was the only piece of evidence he had to support his story.

His dad appeared in the doorway connecting the family room and kitchen. "Can you come in here with us for a few minutes, Chris?" he said. "We want to talk to you about something."

Right away he knew what it must be. They'd found out that he and Pat hadn't gone to the mall today. Light-headed and tight-throated, he got up from the chair and started for the kitchen. "Sure," he said, in what he hoped was an innocent voice. Curiously, his dad smiled as Chris walked past him and sat down at the table across from his mom. His dad joined them.

"Did you find any school clothes at the mall today, Chris?" his mom asked.

The question didn't sound sarcastic. Should he tell her the truth? Now? "No. Nothing I really liked," he said.

"Well, we can go again. Maybe to some other stores," she said.

"Okay," he said. Maybe this wasn't going to be so bad.

"Chris," his dad said, glancing at Chris's mom and back at Chris. He paused, as if trying to put some words together.

*Here it comes*, thought Chris.

"Do you remember what Dr. Wilde told us when we were first going in to see her?" he continued.

Chris thought for a moment. Nothing really stuck out. "Lots of things," he said. "She told us lots of things. I don't remember most of 'em."

"She did tell us lots of things, Chris," his mom said. "And we were having a hard time listening to her back then. Most of what she was telling us we didn't really comprehend or accept. But in the past two days, your dad and I have been talking and thinking about one thing she mentioned that didn't seem like a good idea at the time."

His mom looked embarrassed, hesitant to go on. "What was that?" Chris asked. She smiled but didn't answer, instead glancing at Chris's dad.

"What Dr. Wilde said," his dad began, "was that it might be a good idea for us to consider having another baby soon."

Chris just stared at his dad, trying to comprehend the words, to remember when Dr. Wilde had given that outlandish advice. She couldn't have. But then it came back to him like a bad dream.

"So you're just going to give up on Molly?" he said without thinking.

"Give up on her?" his mom said. "Of course not, Chris. She'll always be with us. We could never forget her, or replace her. We wouldn't try to do that."

"It would be a new life, Chris," his dad said. "Someone for us to care for—to care about. To love." His voice was breaking. "Like we love Molly, but different."

"And we haven't decided anything, Chris," his mom said. Her eyes were shiny, wet. "It's just something we're thinking about. We wanted to know what you think."

Chris's head was spinning. He'd already gone through too much today to deal with anything new. He pushed his chair back from the table, ready to run, but he had to stay. "You really want to know what I think?" He had their attention now. "I think Molly's still alive." He looked from his mom to his dad. They both stared at him. *Crazy. They think I'm crazy,* he thought.

"Why would you say something like that?" his dad asked. He was leaning forward, looking in Chris's eyes, as if trying to get a glimpse of the defective brain cells.

"It's true. I can show you if you'll come into the family room with me."

"Show us what, Chris?" his mom asked.

"The tape. The tape from the day we lost Molly."

"We've seen it," his dad said, sitting back in his

chair, no longer interested. His reaction was short—the final word.

"But it shows Clover telling Molly a secret and Bud and Clover's truck at the park. And the music wasn't even on for most of the time the truck was there, like they suddenly didn't want anybody to know they were around." He took a deep breath, certain that his parents weren't hearing a word he was saying. "They *always* play the music when the truck's at the park," he added. He felt as if he'd just started firing his shots, but he was already out of ammunition. And he hadn't even gotten their attention.

They both stared at him, blank expressions on their faces. His mom tried to smile, but it turned into something else—more of a grimace.

"Bud and Clover?" his dad said, leaning forward again. "What do they have to do with this?"

"They did it, Dad. They took her." He raced into the family room and back, the envelope in his hand, holding it out to his dad, who didn't even look at it. This wasn't the way Chris had planned to do this, but he had to go through with it now. "They left Greenwater and moved to a new place," he said, throwing the envelope on the table. "Three weeks after Molly disappeared, right at the start of the busiest time of the year, they left town. Clover was gone in a few *days*. And nobody knew where they were going."

"They always leave Greenwater for half the year," his dad said. Without really looking at the envelope, he picked it up and held it for a moment, absent-mindedly rubbing his fingers across its surface, before dropping it back on the table address-side down.

Chris couldn't tell if his dad was exasperated or just annoyed, but he decided to go on. "In *June*, Dad?" he said. "Try October."

"I'm sure they had a good reason," his mom said. She looked concerned, as if she were getting ready to get up and give him a hug.

"They said Clover's mom was sick," Chris said.

"Then she probably was," his dad said. He was staring at Chris, as if he didn't quite recognize him.

"They haven't renewed their lease on The Cloverbud," Chris said. "I know they're not coming back to Greenwater. Why would they do that without telling anybody?"

"I don't know, Chris. Why do *you* think they did?" his dad said. "Obviously, Clover's mother couldn't really be sick. After all, she'd probably only be in her seventies or eighties."

Chris could tell by his dad's tone of voice that Chris wasn't even close to convincing him of anything. Exasperated. Definitely exasperated.

But there was no reason to turn back now. "I

think they did it because they took Molly, and they wanted to get out of town before anybody knew they were going or where they were going." He took a deep breath and sat back down.

His dad glanced at his mom, who had her head down. She was wiping at her eyes with the back of her hand.

"And what do you have to base that on, Chris?" his dad said. "A secret Clover told Molly? Their truck being at the park? Their early departure from Greenwater?" He shook his head. "That's nothing, Chris. Do you have any proof?"

"Nothing else," he said, his voice barely audible. "Just what I've told you." Where was Pat, now that he really needed him?

"What about the coloring book?" his dad said. "Do you think it walked out on the dock by itself?"

The coloring book. Chris hadn't thought about Molly's coloring book. How would it have gotten on the dock, unless Molly took it there? He sat looking at his dad and his mom and back at his dad again, but he didn't see their faces—he saw all his hopes fading away to dim, flimsy shadows. Then suddenly he knew—he knew how it got there—and it made him believe more than ever. "Bud took it out on the dock," he said. "He got Molly, and then he took the book out on the dock. He wanted everyone to think she'd fallen in."

"You watch too much television," his dad said.

"We know you miss her, Chris," his mom said. "But we've got to face the fact that Molly died. We all had a good talk about it on Saturday. Let's not go backward now." Her voice was shaky, pleading.

She put her hand over his. He wanted to get up from his chair and drag them in to look at the video-tape, but he was suddenly tired. He couldn't move.

"I have a question for you," his dad said. "How did you get the envelope?"

Chris stared at the wall. "Bud and Clover's mail-box."

"When?"

"Today."

"You were in Greenwater today, Chris?" his mom said. She tightened her grip on his hand. "How did you get there?"

"Bus. Pat and I caught the bus." Why did he feel like a major crime suspect?

"You were supposed to be at the mall, weren't you?" his dad said.

"I knew you wouldn't let me go to the river."

"You're right," his dad said. "It's a long trip by yourself. And there was no reason for you to go."

"I thought there *was*. Now I *know* there was."

"There wasn't," his dad said. His face had gotten flushed. "And I don't want to hear any more about it."

"Why?" Chris said. He could feel his opportunity

slipping away. "What if she's alive? Don't you think there's a chance at least?"

"No," his dad said. His mom was shaking her head.

The doorbell rang. "And I think we need to schedule some more sessions with Dr. Wilde," his dad said.

"I don't want more sessions with Dr. Wilde. I want my sister back."

"We all do, Chris," his mom said.

The doorbell rang again. Chris started to get up, but his legs felt like rubber bands. He sat back down. "Come in, Pat!" he yelled.

The front door opened and closed, and Pat appeared in the kitchen doorway. He looked at the faces at the table and his smile faded. "Did I pick a bad time to come?" he asked. "It looks like Chris just told one of his jokes."

"A bad joke," Chris's dad said.

"Perfect timing," Chris said.

"You told them already?" Pat asked.

"It just came out," Chris said.

"And?"

"They don't believe me."

"But Mr. and Mrs. Barton—" Pat began. His voice trailed off when he looked at their faces. "You should have been there," he continued. "It was strange. Something weird happened. We're sure of it."

"Pat, the only weird thing that happened was that

I couldn't keep my eyes open long enough to keep Molly out of the river," Chris's dad said. He looked at Chris's mom and back at Pat. "We told Chris that we didn't want to hear any more about it. We'd appreciate not hearing any more from you, either." His mouth closed, and his lips formed a thin, grim line on his face.

Chris watched Pat's face redden and his eyes turn liquid. Chris slid his hand out of his mom's grasp, got up, and walked over to him. "Don't worry about it," he said softly. "It's my fault. I got you into this."

"What if something had happened to you guys today?" his mom said. "You were a hundred miles away from home, and we had no idea where you were."

"We couldn't tell you," Chris said. "Dad already said you wouldn't have let us go."

"And I don't want you pulling anything like that again," his dad said. "We've always trusted you and treated you as a responsible person. You've earned our trust. I don't want that to change."

Chris wanted to say something, to tell them they were wrong. But were they? He wasn't as sure now. And his dad's face said that the conversation was over.

"Understood?" his dad said.

Chris looked at him and then at his mom. Her expression was begging him to say yes. "Okay," he said. Pat nodded in agreement. They glanced at each other and back at Chris's parents. Chris wasn't sure what they were supposed to do next.

"Do you want some dessert, Pat?" Chris's mom asked, as if the discussion had never occurred. Her voice was near normal now, but forced, hollow.

"No thanks, Mrs. B.," Pat said. "I've got to get going."

"Another time, then," Chris's mom said.

"Sure."

Chris walked him to the door and returned to the kitchen. His parents looked up at him in surprise, their quiet discussion interrupted. *Probably talking about me*, Chris thought. *Probably thought I'd go to my room like a spanked puppy.*

"You guys can have another baby if you want to," he said, "but don't plan on moving it into Molly's room. She's going to need it when she comes home."

"Chris—" his dad began. But Chris turned and hurried away, running from the hurt in their eyes, taking the stairs three at a time, closing his door behind him.

An hour later he lay in the dark. He felt drained, tired to the bone, but not sleepy. The day had seemed a week long, and everything that had happened was rerunning itself through his mind.

It had all been going in the right direction until the discussion in the kitchen. Then disaster—and doubt. He'd had doubts all along, but his mom and dad not believing him, not even giving him a chance to explain, had made those doubts bigger. Even Pat hadn't had the heart to stand up to Chris's parents. Had Pat really believed at all? Or was he just going along with it to humor his friend?

Chris wasn't sure of anything anymore. Maybe he'd been kidding himself the whole time. If he had, he should just give up on this crazy idea and get on with his life. But if he hadn't, how was he going to see to it that Molly got on with *her* life? Who would help—the police? If his own parents didn't believe him? He didn't think so.

Who, then? Where were all the heroes? Batman would have believed a kid's story. Sherlock Holmes would have come all the way from London to help out. But where were the *real* heroes?

Chris couldn't think of any—none that he could talk to, anyway. He rolled and crept across his bed, sweating in the warm night air. When he finally fell asleep, he dreamed of Molly. She stood in front of him on the beach, toeing the hot sand and laughing up at him. Then she turned and took off toward the dock, running like a tiny race horse, her feet kicking up little golden-brown roostertails. He sprinted after her, but she was too fast for him. A hundred yards away, she stopped at the foot of the dock and waved. Then she ran for the woods.

**CHRIS** woke up feeling heroic. He didn't know why. Maybe it helped that it was dark. He couldn't see that he still had the same kid-sized body, that he was still only thirteen years old. But he knew that if a hero was needed, he was going to have to be that hero. There *was* a need; Molly was alive and alone in a faraway town. And there was only one person who believed it, who knew where she was and was willing to go after her: him. And maybe Pat. He had to talk to Pat.

He looked at his clock—4:23. Too early to call anyone. But he was wide awake now, his mind racing down dark paths.

He switched on his lamp, walked to the desk, and pulled a volume of the encyclopedia set from the shelf. He opened it to "Florida." A map showed cities and counties, lakes and rivers, highways and roads. It took him a while, but he finally spotted New Moon Bay. Westview was just north of it. Using the scale on the map and a ruler, he figured the distance at about thirty miles. Thirty miles of western Florida coastline. The nearest big city was probably Tampa, a hundred miles or so to the south of Westview.

He pulled another book from the shelf and opened it to "United States." The U.S. map was familiar, but he'd never really figured distances between states before. As he picked up his ruler something clicked against his window. He half-turned in the chair and looked, but his shade was pulled down. Nothing there. An early morning breeze through the partially open window nudged the shade into the frame. A quiet click. He turned back to the desk.

Another click, louder, not the wind. He walked to the window, pushed the shade a crack open, and looked outside. Down on the front lawn, ready to throw a small twig, was Pat. Chris raised the shade and stuck his head out the window.

"Pat! What are you doing?" he whispered loudly.

"I couldn't sleep. I saw your light come on. Let me in the back door—I've gotta talk to you."

Chris slipped quietly downstairs and then tiptoed back up with Pat on his heels. The house was dark and still and cool. Chris closed his door quietly behind them and sat down in his desk chair. Pat leaned against the desk and pulled a wrinkled piece of paper from his pocket.

"I did some calling after I got home last night," Pat said.

"Did you find a shrink for me?"

"I don't think you're crazy, Chris. I was calling the airlines."

"Going somewhere?"

"Look, I'm sorry I wasn't more help last night, but it was pretty much all over by the time I got there. Your parents weren't about to listen to me."

"I know—I'm sorry. I'm just upset that they didn't believe us, not even a little."

"Maybe they're afraid," Pat said. "Aren't you?"

"Yeah."

"Anyway, after I left last night I figured that we're the only ones Molly has left to help her. So we need to do something."

Chris had to smile. He could see Pat getting wound up. He'd started pacing around the room. "So you called the airlines?"

"Yeah, about ten of 'em. I didn't know which ones went where. But I finally got the information we need." He handed Chris the paper.

"You mean you want to go with me to Florida? You really do believe she's alive?"

"No. I just figured I'd blow four hundred twenty

dollars on a trip to Westview to humor a crazy friend."

"What?" Chris said. "It costs that much? Do you even have four hundred twenty dollars?" He pulled open the desk drawer, searching for his bank book, but it was hidden somewhere in the debris.

"In my bank account. More than that, actually."

"Me, too," Chris said. He'd been sticking money in there since he was a little kid.

"Can you get it out without your parents' okay?" Pat asked.

"I have before," Chris said. "You?" He got up and walked to his door, listening for his parents, but there was no sound from their room.

"Yeah," Pat said. "So you were already planning on going?"

"I'd decided this morning, when I woke up."

"Alone?" Pat's face suddenly drooped in the soft light from the desk lamp.

"I was going to call you. I didn't know if you'd want to go. We're definitely going to get in trouble with our parents." Chris sat down on the corner of his bed.

"Not if we find Molly."

The thought shot through Chris like a lightning bolt. His hair felt as if it were electrified, standing on end. He ran his hand through it, expecting to see sparks. He got up and wandered around the room, studying the piece of paper Pat had given him.

Pat stopped pacing and watched him crisscross the rug aimlessly. "Remember when Molly started calling me Patty and I told you I didn't like it?"

"Yeah?" Chris said.

"I never told her to stop," Pat said.

"Why?"

"I liked it. I want her to call me Patty again."

Chris suddenly wondered what it would be like not to have Pat for a friend. He took a deep breath and let it out slowly. "Look at those encyclopedias on the desk, Pat," he said.

Pat glanced at the open books. "I already looked at my atlas," he said. "That's how I knew what airport we'd fly into. It's Tampa."

Chris didn't respond. He sat down on the edge of the bed, still staring at the paper. Finally he looked up at Pat. "I don't think we should go today or tomorrow," he said.

"Why not?"

"My parents are going to be on the alert after yesterday. They may not let me out of the house. And you won't be any better off, if your folks get told. But after a couple of days, they'll probably think we gave up on the whole idea." He stared at the wall. "And we've still got to get our money, buy the tickets, and make our plans. That's going to take a little time."

"I guess you're right. I don't think Clover and Bud are going anywhere."

Chris looked at the paper again. "You've got a Central Express flight showing here that leaves at 9:30 a.m. Is that every day?"

"All of 'em are daily."

"That looks like a good one. We'd be able to leave for the airport after our parents go to work and still get there in time to catch the plane."

"You think they'll let us on by ourselves?" Pat said. "Or even sell us the tickets?"

Chris hadn't thought about that—about being too young. He'd just figured if they had the money, they could go. But now he wasn't so sure. "I don't know," he said. "We'll have to try it and see." He wasn't going to let any silly airline regulations wreck their plans. If he and Pat had to, they'd ride the bus all the way to Florida.

"Right," Pat said. "What about coming back? When do we schedule the return flight? If we don't get round-trip tickets up here, it costs a lot more."

"More than four hundred twenty dollars?" Chris said. Maybe they *should* take the bus. But that would take time—possibly enough time for his parents to track them down and stop them. The plane had to be their first choice. "We could probably come back Monday or Tuesday," he said. "That should do it, but there's no way we can know for sure." He thought a moment, rubbing his eyes. "If we find her, we'll have to go to the police down there."

"If they have police."

"Every place has police."

"Even Westview?"

"Even Westview." But what kind of police? Chris wasn't sure. He had an image of a fat guy with a flat-brimmed hat and sunglasses, who called everyone "boy." But they'd have to worry about the police later.

"So what do we do now?" Pat asked.

Chris glanced at the clock. "You're going to have to leave. My dad will be up soon for his morning run. By eight o'clock they'll both be gone to work and your parents will be out of your house, too. Come back then."

"To make plans?"

"Right," Chris said, walking to the bedroom door with Pat. Neither of them spoke on the way downstairs. Chris opened the back door silently and let Pat out into the cool morning air. The sky was brightening in the east.

"Pat," Chris whispered as Pat started for home.

Pat turned around. Chris could just make out his features in the early dawn's dim light. A smile had spread across his face. He looked excited, glowing, reflecting Chris's own feelings. "Yeah?" he whispered.

"Thanks for coming," Chris said, and slipped back inside.

**CHRIS'S** parents asked him his plans for the day, but put no restrictions on him. They were surprised to see him up early again, but didn't seem suspicious. Maybe they were just doing a good job of covering up. Or maybe Chris taking off on another adventure was the last thing on their minds. He wasn't sure.

But at nine o'clock his mom called him from work: just checking to see how he was doing. He told her he and Pat would be going to the park soon to throw the football around. At nine-fifteen his dad called. Chris told him the same thing.

By then Chris had decided that they *were* suspicious, and he and Pat had made their plans for the day. By nine-thirty they were on their bikes, football and bank books in Chris's backpack.

The excitement Chris had felt early in the morning had partly given way to nervousness and fear and doubt. He glanced at Pat, searching for some of the same emotions, as they pedalled along side by side. "How are you feeling?" he asked.

"Fine," Pat said. "I'm not sick or anything."

"No, I mean your mind. Are you nervous?"

"Of course. This ain't exactly like our little trip to Greenwater, and that made me nervous. How about you?"

"Yeah, me, too," Chris said. "You heard my dad's lecture on how they've always trusted me. They really have. But today they probably don't, quite as much. After this, who knows? Maybe not at all. But I mostly think we're doing the right thing."

"It's something we have to do," Pat said. "We need to keep telling ourselves that, or this is going to be a lot harder."

They went to the bank first. At the teller's window, they had a loud and continuous conversation with each other about the great racing bikes they were going to buy, and how the bikes were going to be worth every penny of the money they were withdrawing. But the teller didn't seem to be particularly interested in bikes or concerned about the amount of the withdrawals. They walked out of the bank with six one-hundred-dollar bills and ten twenty-dollar bills each, surprised at how easy it had been, and headed for the mall, where the closest travel agency was.

Chris grew more nervous as they went into the travel agency. What if you *did* have to be a certain age to buy tickets? But they tried to be calm, matter-of-fact, even when they gave the young woman phony names that they'd decided to use only minutes before. She seemed only slightly curious, and without hesitating, sold them round-trip tickets to Tampa— for flights departing Thursday at 9:30 and returning Tuesday at 5:00—for $420 each. They figured that they still had $380 each for expenses. In the back of his mind, Chris was thinking that should leave enough to buy a return ticket for a little girl, too. But he didn't let the thought get too far out in the open. He believed more than anything that Molly was alive, but in the light of day, the idea of finding her and bringing her back home would still have some warts on it, like a fat toad that only held the promise of really being a prince.

After buying the tickets, Chris and Pat biked to the library. They located a large atlas and photo-copied a detailed map of Florida. Chris folded it carefully and stuck it in his backpack. Looking up, he noticed Pat nervously gazing around the big, quiet, sparsely occupied room.

"What's the matter, Pat?" he asked.

"I don't know," Pat said, "but don't you get the feeling that everybody's watching us—that they all know what's going on?"

"Like they're all spies sent by my parents?"

"Or mine."

"You really think so?"

"They're parents, aren't they?"

Chris didn't answer. His attention had shifted to a rumpled-looking man reading at a table across the room. Every few seconds he would glance up at the boys and then go back to his book.

Pat followed Chris's gaze. "A spy?" he whispered as the man looked up and then quickly back down again.

Chris stared at the man, waiting for him to look up again. He did, smiling this time, a lifeless, unnatural grin that turned Chris's stomach. "I don't think our parents know anyone like that," he said under his breath.

Pat turned and headed for the door. "Let's go," he said.

Chris followed him, not looking back. Suddenly he didn't feel very good about what they were planning. The man at the table had reminded him that two kids on their own could encounter people and situations that might be tough to handle. And when they were a thousand miles from home, who would help? He tried to push the thought out of his mind. *There are good people, too,* he said to himself, looking up and down the sidewalk for a friendly face.

He had to wait until they reached the bike rack. A pretty young woman in a Notre Dame T-shirt walked by and smiled at them. They turned and watched her go into the library.

Pat grinned at him. "She was smiling at *me,* Chris," he said.

"In your dreams," Chris said. They got on their bikes and started for home.

Once they arrived at Chris's house, they grabbed some lemonade from the refrigerator and headed for the backyard, where they pulled out the map, going over every inch of Florida's west coast until they were both familiar with it.

"Now all we have to do is figure out how to get around down there," Pat said.

"There must be buses," Chris said. "And we can take a taxi to the bus depot, if we have to. I think we've got enough in our budget."

"Maybe we should just rent a limo."

"I'll tell you something," Chris said. "If we really pull this off, if we bring Molly back with us, I bet my folks will get us the biggest limo around for the trip home from the airport."

"We're gonna bring her back," Pat said. "No problem." But his nervous grin gave him away. Chris knew that his friend was having some doubts.

The next day and a half dragged by. The boys checked on bus schedules from home to downtown and from downtown to the airport. They each packed a change of clothes in their backpacks. Then they waited, and played catch with the football, and talked, and tried not to look suspicious. But mostly they waited, with the burden of what they were about to do growing heavier on their minds.

**THE** small, dark-haired girl slipped from under the quilt and off the high double bed, her feet landing softly on the thick carpet. She turned to look at Antkova, sleeping soundlessly on the other side of the bed, the covers slowly rising and falling with each breath.

Across the room, the drawn window shade shifted in the afternoon breeze, allowing in a sliver of bright sunshine. The little girl tiptoed to the window and held the shade an inch away from the frame, squinting out at the daylight and the small backyard with its high wooden fence.

She wished she could go outside and play, or just lie down on the grass with her dolly and take a nap in the warm sun. She felt tired, but she couldn't fall asleep on the big bed. The dreams would come again—dreams of faces and places that were growing fuzzy now—and she would wake up crying.

Antkova stirred in her sleep, reaching out an arm to the space where the little girl had lain a few moments before. Her hand aimlessly explored the empty spot and then dropped onto the bed and froze. The girl watched wide-eyed, holding her breath. She wanted her to sleep some more. She wanted to look into the big mirror again.

She waited until she thought there would be no more movement on the bed, and then let out a quiet sigh and crept over to the dresser. As she struggled onto the stool, her elbow bumped an earring and pro-pelled it against the picture on the back of the table—the picture in the flowery pink frame of Antkova—a younger, thinner Antkova—and a pretty lady holding a little baby on her lap. The noise was loud, real loud, and she turned quickly to look toward the bed. But the head covered with curly red hair stayed on the pillow, the eyes remained closed, and the covers didn't move.

The little girl pushed herself up onto her knees and expertly pivoted around toward the wall and the big vanity mirror. She'd known that she wouldn't look the same—she hadn't looked the same all the other times she'd done this—but the face that stared back at her still seemed to belong to somebody else. She quickly glanced over her shoulder to see who it was, but there was no one between her and the bed. *It's me*, she thought. *It's my face.*

She turned back to the mirror and tried to remember how she'd looked before. Different. When it was the yesterdays before yesterdays, when she'd lived with her mommy and daddy and Kis, before she'd come to this place, she'd looked different. Her face looked thinner now, and she could see her ears. Her hair was short, and changed—a different color. Dark, like her eyes. Not blond, like her mommy used to say, or white, like Kis said when he teased her. Then she remembered her favorite poem, the one she knew because her daddy had said it for her whenever he came into her room in the morning to wake her and get her dressed. She closed her eyes and tried to picture his face as his mouth formed the words. She recited them softly to herself, her lips barely moving.

My little girl with golden hair
Awakes to find me standing there,
A bit of sleep still in her eyes,
My little girl, my sweet surprise.

She ran her fingers slowly through her hair and looked at her hand, expecting to see it, too, had turned dark. But when she held it up in the dim light and examined it on both sides, it looked the same as always. She decided that the stuff in Antkova's bottle must only work on hair. And it made her hair look funny. It made *her* look funny.

She thought of the first time she'd seen herself like this. It wasn't in this mirror—not in any mirror. She'd fallen asleep, crying, in Antkova's bed, in the house behind the ice cream store, and awakened in her new car seat, with Antkova sitting next to her behind the steering wheel. She looked out the window at the darkness. The camper truck was moving fast down the road, and she couldn't see anything but shapes and shadows and faraway lights, but in the shiny dark glass, she could see a reflection—someone she didn't know. The face looked sad and frightened—just like she felt—but the hair was short and dark. Then she thought about the night before, and Antkova's scissors, and the stuff in the bottle, and she knew who was looking back at her from the window. She stared at her reflection until it disappeared in the light from the morning sun. Then she fell asleep. That night, and the night after that, and the night after that, she looked into that same glass and saw the same reflection, while Antkova kept driving.

Now tears glistened in her eyes as she peered into the dresser mirror again. She imagined her mommy standing behind her, looking down at her, but not knowing who she was. "It's me, Mommy," she said softly. "It's really me. I'll show you."

She reached across the dresser top and carefully

picked up a round ceramic box with both hands. Its top shifted as she set it down in front of her, and a small cloud of powder puffed out, leaving off-white specks on the dark surface of the table. She removed the lid and lowered it gently onto the shiny wood. More powder fell from the edges of the top, making a circle where it sat.

The powder puff felt soft in her hand as she lifted it out of the box, and so light she thought it might float away like the little specks of dust dancing in the air. Like a magic carpet that would carry her far away to her real house and her mom and dad and Kis. But she held it firmly between her thumb and fingers and slowly brought it up to her hair. Looking intently into the mirror, she patted her head with the puff and smiled when the spot turned white. She continued patting, dipping into the box, and patting again, until all of her hair, and most of her face, was white.

"See, Mommy?" she whispered as she stared at her reflection. But the hair didn't look quite right and her face was too pale. Her eyes were red from crying and from that powder. She looked like a ghost. Wouldn't she ever be herself again? How would Mommy and Daddy and Kis know her when they came to get her?

She took a deep breath, and powder sifted off her hair and into her nose. She felt a sneeze building and tried to stop it with a finger to her upper lip like Kis used to do. But it didn't work; she sneezed loudly three times in a row, her head rocking back and forth and sending clouds of powder into the air. Propelled by the force of her sneeze, more powder mushroomed out of the box in front of her and formed a thin layer of snow on the dresser.

She looked up into the mirror. A face had appeared behind her. A nice, smiling face with sad eyes. Antkova was awake now, standing in back of her, close enough that the little girl could feel her warm breath.

"Are you okay, honey?" Antkova asked. She put a hand on the powdery shoulder of the little girl, who looked at the picture on the dresser—the picture of Antkova with her hand on the shoulder of the pretty lady. The little girl began to shiver in the warm room.

"Yes," she said. "I just had to sneeze. The powder got in my nose."

"Well, I can see that it would. You know, you shouldn't play with Aunt Clover's things, dear. Now we're going to have to clean up this mess and give you a bath."

"I'm sorry, Antkova," she said, lifting her head and turning to look up at the stocky woman in the flowery blue dress. More powder drifted down from her head.

"Don't you like your hair, honey?"

The little girl looked at the floor and slowly shook

her head.

"Well, it won't have to be this way always. You can have your pretty blond hair back in a while."

"Before my mommy and daddy come and get me? They might not know I'm their little girl if I'm wearing this hair."

Antkova looked down at her with her sad-eyed smile. "It'll be before that, honey." She knelt down next to the stool and gave the little girl a hug, powder rubbing off on her face and hair and dress. "It'll be before that."

**14**

**THURSDAY** morning came early for Chris. It was still dark in his room when he woke from a series of short, restless naps, his stomach in a knot. He felt as if he were facing a day or several days that could turn out to be either like Christmas or a trip to the dentist to have every tooth in his mouth pulled, without novocaine. There probably wouldn't be any in-between. They'd either find her or they'd find out how foolish they'd been. He didn't even want to think about the kinds of trouble they could get in on the way to either alternative. And then they'd have to come back and face their parents—if they made it back.

He looked at the clock—5:07. He'd hoped it was later. He wondered if Pat was awake yet and decided he must be. Pat's nerves had been showing through his skin last night as they'd paced around the neighborhood like two cats with their fur on fire. Chris had figured then that neither of them would get much sleep, although he knew they both needed it.

Now he had to lie here and stare at the ceiling for the next two hours. He couldn't risk getting up, not yet. A suspicious mom and dad was the last thing he needed.

Two hours later, he sat at his desk listening to his parents' hushed voices drifting up the stairs. He signed "Love, Chris," at the bottom of the note he'd just written, and read it silently to himself.

"Dear Mom and Dad," it began.

> Pat and I have gone to look for Molly. We think we know where she is. We think she's not at the bottom of the river. It shouldn't take long to find out if we're right. We'll be back in a couple of days. Watch the videotape again. Think about what we told you. It's spooky. We have to check it out, but we'll be careful. I'll call you.

It looked about right. Enough information but not too much. He didn't want people chasing after them before he and Pat had a chance to find out what they needed to find out. He folded the note in thirds, wrote "Mom and Dad" on the outside, and tucked it into the desk drawer.

His parents looked up at him and smiled when he walked into the kitchen. Surprised but not suspicious. *Good,* he thought. He'd considered staying in his bedroom until after they left for work so their suspicions wouldn't get stirred up, but he wanted to see them. He needed to see them.

"What's up, Chris?" his dad asked.

*What does he mean by that?* Chris thought.

"Nothing much," he said. "Some barking dog woke me up and I couldn't get back to sleep. Then I smelled food down here." He eyed the omelette and cantaloupe sitting on his mom's plate.

"This is mine, you little beggar," she said, smiling and grabbing onto her plate with both hands as if Chris were going to pounce on it from ten feet away.

His dad laughed. "I'll make you one, too, Chris," he said, getting up from the table. "I don't think you're going to talk your mom out of hers."

A half-hour later Chris watched them pull out of the driveway. Pat's parents would have left a few minutes earlier. They always did.

Chris was waiting outside the front door when Pat arrived five minutes later, red-faced and out of breath.

"You ready?" Pat asked.

"I think so," Chris said. He'd left the note in the middle of the kitchen table.

"Tickets? Money? Map? Clothes?" Pat said.

Chris nodded. The tickets and clothes were in the backpack. He'd split the money up between his wallet, his socks, and the backpack's zippered inside pocket. "How about you? You got everything—your money, change for bus fare?"

"I checked about ten times," Pat said.

"Did you leave your parents a note?"

"Yeah," Pat replied, swallowing hard. "I told them what but not where."

Chris checked the front door to make sure it was locked. "Let's go, then," he said, looking at his watch. "We've only got about ten minutes before the next bus."

They left the yard at a fast walk. Two boys in T-shirts and jeans, each with a small pack on his back, looking as if they were heading off to the park for the day.

They covered the three blocks to the bus stop in a hurry. The bus was crowded with people on their way to work downtown. Chris stood in the aisle next to Pat and watched people napping over the morning paper. He imagined the headlines reading, "LOCAL BOYS MISSING, FEARED DEAD." A shudder shot through him. He looked at Pat for comfort, but Pat was in a world of his own, his eyes darting around the bus.

"Looking for spies again, Pat?" he asked softly.

"These people are just pretending to be going to work," Pat whispered with a nervous grin. "We both know they're spies, and who they're following."

"I don't think they'd follow us very fast," Chris said. "They look like they're in a coma."

"They're pretending."

Chris nodded toward the two-person seat next to Pat, where a fat woman sat by herself. She was slumped over in the seat with her eyes closed, breathing heavily, a magazine propped up over one side of her face to block out the sun.

"She's doing a good job of pretending," Chris said, and they both laughed. None of the other passengers even looked up.

Once downtown, they made a quick connection with the bus to Mitchell Field. It wasn't as crowded, and they found seats toward the back. Looking out the window, Chris was reminded of the trip to Greenwater. It already seemed like a long time ago.

Chris and Pat had both been to the airport with their parents before, but they agreed that it seemed bigger now and less friendly. They found the Central Express ticketing area and looked on the overhead monitor to check for flight 151 to Tampa. It was departing on time from gate 22. Since they already had their tickets and they had no baggage to check, they skipped the line at the ticket counter and headed for the gate.

Five minutes later they'd gone through the security area and were standing at the check-in counter for flight 151. So far so good, but Chris's nerves were telling him otherwise. He felt as if he were five years old again in a classroom full of strangers, on his first day of school, watching his mom walk away and leave him.

"Do you gentlemen have a seating preference?" the young man behind the counter asked as Chris handed him the tickets. His name tag said Jay Miller.

Chris wasn't sure what that meant. He waited for Pat to say something, but Pat didn't seem to know what the guy was talking about, either. Pat looked at Chris. "I don't know," he said. "Do you have one?"

"Not really," Chris said, glancing back at Jay Miller, who looked amused.

"We're not very full this morning," Jay Miller said, checking his computer. "I can give you window seats, aisle seats—just about anything you want. What sounds good?"

"A window," Chris said. He wanted to see where they were going.

"Just put me next to him," Pat said.

"Row nineteen okay?" Jay Miller said, grinning.

"Sure," Pat said.

Chris had no idea where row 19 was, and he doubted that Pat did, either, but at least they were about finished. Jay Miller seemed like a nice guy, but his smile was making Chris even more nervous.

"So, which one of you is Rocky Sims?" Jay Miller said, his pen poised over the ticket packet. Pat hesitated and then held out his hand for the ticket and boarding pass.

"Not sure, huh?" Jay Miller said, still grinning. He marked the seat number on the pass and handed the packet to Pat.

*Keep smiling,* Chris thought. *Keep thinking we're just a couple of ignorant kids.* "He just daydreams a lot," Chris said, reaching for the other ticket folder. "Let's go, Rocky." They headed for seats by the big window where they could watch the planes take off and land.

"Have a good flight," Jay Miller called after them.

"Thanks," they both replied.

Chris was shaking his head as they sat down. "Rocky Sims," he said under his breath. "What a dumb name. And the least you could do is recognize it when somebody talks to you."

"I like it," Pat said indignantly. "And besides, I was nervous."

"About what?" Chris said, trying to sound calm.

"You know why, *Fred,*" Pat said, lowering his voice. "Speaking of dumb names. *Fred Barnes.*"

"Can I help it if I grew up watching The Flintstones?" Chris whispered. "It's good enough to keep people off our tails if they decide to check the airlines." Chris hoped it would be, anyway—at least for a few days.

Chris watched Pat rummage through his backpack and pull out two bananas. He offered one to Chris, who shook his head no. His stomach was full of butterflies, and they were getting more active. Planning this trip had brought out one set of emotions; actually going on it was allowing a different group to surface. Fear and doubt were right up near the top.

The big plane was only half-full. Pat and Chris's seats were midway back on the right side. There were no passengers in the six other seats in their row, which stretched across the plane and was divided by two aisles. Chris was glad for the space. He hadn't been looking forward to lying to more people about where they were going and why.

He was thinking of the "why" part when the plane inched away from the terminal. He watched Pat check his seat belt and grip the arm rests. "Don't fall out," he said to him in his most sincere voice. Pat ignored him. Chris went back to his thinking, looking out the window at the pavement drifting slowly past.

Suddenly they were accelerating down the runway. A moment later they lifted off. The plane gained altitude and banked to the right, and for an instant Chris felt as if they were about to slide back to earth. But then the plane righted itself and continued up.

Below him Chris saw the city, and then it was gone, and they were climbing through cottonball clouds. And he was thinking—still thinking about why they were going. He figured that he'd stay focused on that—on finding Molly and bringing her back—and he'd be able to keep the feeling in the pit of his stomach under control. If he could just concentrate on where they were going, the journey there might not seem so scary. But right now he was scared—not only of what lay ahead, but also of what he'd left behind. What were his parents going to think? What were they going to feel?

He looked down at a puffy blanket of clouds—and suddenly he felt exhausted. Suddenly he couldn't keep his eyes open. He let them close, and drifted off, still thinking about Molly.

"Chris," he heard someone say through a fog. He opened his eyes and glanced around, not sure where he was at first. Then he remembered. He looked at Pat, who was staring at him with a funny expression on his face. "Did you say something?" Chris said.

"You been in a trance?" Pat asked. "I tried talking to you a couple of times before I figured out you were asleep. You tired?"

"Just thinking," Chris said. "What did you say?"

"Nothing much. I was just saying that things are going okay so far. I mean, we made it on the plane and everything. I think it's even the right plane."

"I hope so," Chris said. Pat was right. So far, things had gone okay. So far, they'd been able to avoid trouble. He wondered how long that would last.

He looked up to see the flight attendants approaching with a cart. He didn't feel hungry, but he might as well try to eat something. He wasn't sure when they'd get another chance, and this food was already paid for.

They ate their meal quietly. Chris picked at his food and stared at the countryside flowing by far below: serpentine rivers; straight-arrow highways crisscrossing in perfect cloverleafs; forests and lakes; mile after mile of brown and green fields in squares and rectangles and circles; and here and there a small town or a range of hills rising above the plain.

After the flight attendant took the remains of their food, the boys lay back in their seats and dozed off. When Chris jump-started himself awake, the plane was in its descent. But a dream had awakened him, a dream of Molly standing in a green rectangular field and waving to him. He looked out the window. The terrain had changed. There were no more fields—not the same kind, anyway. The ground below looked green and boggy, and lakes and swamps and narrow paths of water dotted and striped the land. Florida. Somewhere over Florida.

**THE** air outside the air-conditioned terminal was familiar but different. Still humid. But thicker, heavier. And the afternoon heat lay on them like a sponge.

They located the ground transportation booth and learned from the woman behind the counter that they could get on a van to the bus depot, where they would be able to catch a bus to just about anywhere they wanted to go. She let them use her phone to call the depot, and for an instant Chris imagined himself asking if there was a bus leaving for Milwaukee that afternoon. He thought about how much easier it would be just to get on the bus and head for home, and not have to face whatever was ahead of them. But it was only a thought; he concentrated on Molly again, discarding the idea of skipping out as if it were chocolate-covered liver, and asked the man on the phone about the bus to Westview. They could easily catch the next one, he said, which departed at 3:30.

No one in the group of people waiting for the vans seemed to pay much attention to them. Chris guessed that kids on their own at a Florida airport were no big deal. But he was glad when the van arrived. He found himself worrying that something would happen to mess up their plans.

An old lady and a middle-aged couple got in the van with them. The couple got out first, at a high-rise hotel. The old lady turned to look at Chris and Pat as the van got back on the road. She faced frontward again, but Chris knew something was on her mind. He looked out the window, pretending to ignore her. She turned around again.

"You boys going to the bus depot?" she asked.

Chris looked at Pat, who was faking sleep. "Yes," he said.

"Where you off to?"

"Westview," Chris said.

"Westview," she said, drawing the name out musically. "I know people in Westview. Used to visit there when my husband was alive. Good fishing there." She nodded her head slightly, as if registering a long-ago memory. "Have you lived there long?"

What was this, twenty questions? Chris was hoping for some time to think. "Just visiting," he said. He looked out the window again, wishing she'd take the hint. There wasn't a mountain or hill or even a high spot in sight. It was flat—the flattest place he'd ever seen. A good place to ride a bike, he decided, but not quite what he'd envisioned. He could see palm trees—he'd expected to see those—but they were bigger, more unreal, than he'd imagined, and the houses were smaller. Except for some big homes near the hotel, he'd seen mostly small stucco boxes in rows of faded pink and yellow, lining each side of the streets. Many of the bigger streets were cluttered with convenience stores, fast-food restaurants, and gas stations. He decided that they hadn't seen the best part of town.

"Who are you visiting there?" Every time she said "there" it came out "they-uh."

"My aunt and uncle."

"Oh," she said thoughtfully. "What is they-uh name?"

Chris thought for a moment. "Smith," he said finally. Something original.

"Don't know any Smiths," she said.

"Oh," Chris said, hoping she didn't know everybody in the town.

The van crossed a busy intersection and pulled up in front of the bus depot. Pat woke up miraculously as the driver slid the side door open for them, allowing a wave of hot air to flood into the van and give them a taste of what waited for them outside. They got out reluctantly, paid him, and started for the entrance. Chris had thought about giving him a tip, but he didn't know if he was supposed to, or how much to give. Besides, he was still having a hard time believing that it cost them ten dollars each to get here. But the lady at the airport had told them that a taxi would be more than that. He wondered how long their money was going to last them.

"You boys have a nice trip," the old lady called to them before the door slammed shut.

Chris and Pat turned and waved toward the van. The old lady smiled at them through the window as the van drove off.

"Thanks for your help, Sleepy," Chris said.

"You were handling things okay," Pat said sheepishly. "I didn't want to mess up your story. Besides, I think she liked you."

"She liked the company."

A half-hour later they were on the bus for Westview and points north. Except for a white-haired couple near the front and two college-age girls in the middle of the bus, Chris and Pat were the only passengers. They sat in the back.

"I wonder how this bus company makes any money," Pat said.

Chris shrugged. All he could think about now was

their destination, what they were going to do when they got there, what they'd find. It seemed as if it had been a year since they'd gotten on the bus to Greenwater. Now the final leg of their tour was almost over. Suddenly two more hours didn't seem long enough. What if they'd been wrong? There'd be no more hope. All the suspicions would be washed away. The only thing left would be crushing disappointment, and a long trip home to angry parents.

He looked out and watched business districts transforming themselves into neighborhoods with houses and yards—bigger, nicer houses and yards with swimming pools and lots of palm trees and strange-looking shrubs and flowers. More like the Florida he'd seen pictures of. They were on a main road now, picking up speed as the afternoon traffic thinned out. Except for trees and buildings, the terrain was still flat in every direction.

"It's going to be late by the time we get there," Chris said. "I think we should try to check into a motel and start looking around tomorrow." He hoped they could get a motel. What if there weren't any in Westview, or if none of them had a vacancy? What if they wouldn't rent a room to a couple of kids? He and Pat should have called down here ahead of time, he decided, but it was too late now.

Pat shot him a questioning look. "Why wait to start looking?" he said. "We can get a motel room and then check things out. It'll still be light for quite a while."

Chris looked at his watch. Not yet four, and he'd already set it to Eastern time. Pat was right. "Okay," he said. "I guess I'm trying to put things off. But we need to be careful. We can't let Bud and Clover know we're in town—not yet." He got out his wallet and took a long look at Molly's picture, at her smiling face. Wondering if she was smiling now, he put the wallet back in his pants pocket.

"So what's the plan, Sherlock?" Pat asked. "You got any ideas? You think we can get a motel room?"

Chris stared out the window for a long moment. Pat seemed more relaxed than he'd been earlier in the day, and Chris wished some of that would rub off on him—that he'd feel better, too. But at least he wasn't feeling any worse. That knot in his stomach could be getting bigger and tighter with every mile they traveled along this highway. Instead it was just sitting there, letting him know that this wasn't just an adventure they were on.

"No real plan, I guess, Pat," he said finally, ignoring Pat's concern about the motel. "I thought we'd call information and try to get the addresses for the store and house, and then find them—without being seen."

"And get into their house if we have to," Pat said.

"Yeah, somehow, without looking suspicious.

Without getting caught. And then get back out with Molly, or convince the police to get her out. No problem."

"Not for us," Pat said.

Chris got the impression that Pat really meant it. And why not? They weren't coming all the way down here to get discouraged or cowardly at the last minute. He couldn't think of anything he wouldn't do to get Molly back. But he hadn't been tested yet.

Outside, the terrain had become long stretches of green foliage interrupted by patches of swampy water and an occasional side road. The palm trees stood in clumps and rows now, appearing like something from a postcard, but Chris was surprised by the big, long-needled pines lining the highway. They looked out of place, anchored in the marshy ground. He stared out toward the horizon—still flat for as far as he could see—where the blue sky met the earth and turned almost white in the afternoon haze. He couldn't see any houses—or buildings of any kind—and he imagined what it would be like to be out there in that great, green stretch of water meadow in the heat of the day.

Pat leaned over and peered out at the countryside passing by. "Let's make sure we can get a motel room," he said. "There's no way I'm sleeping in a field with alligators and snakes." He folded his arms across his chest.

That was fine with Chris. He'd never been fond of snakes. And he wasn't anxious to get acquainted with any alligators.

The bus exited the main highway three times to make stops in small coastal towns. They could see water and beaches, and Chris wondered what it would be like to swim in that water, to run along those beaches. He'd never been to the ocean before. But this wasn't the day to find out.

The fourth time the bus stopped, the town was New Moon Bay. They were getting close. They spent the rest of the trip on the edges of their seats.

"This has to be it," Pat said as the bus slowed and turned off again. A flat road winding through shallow marshes, green trees, and thick undergrowth brought them to the sign for Westview a few moments later. Population 1,972, it said. Somebody had blasted it with a shotgun.

The only indication of a town was a few mossy mobile homes tucked back in the trees. A three-legged dog stood sentinel by an old rusted pickup. In an overgrown yard, a thin boy about Chris's size threw a dirty baseball into the air and caught it bare-handed. He stared at the bus as it roared past. Chris involuntarily slumped down in his seat.

"You'd think that guy had never seen this bus come by before," Pat said.

"Maybe it's the main attraction in this town."

"I don't think so," Pat said. "I think the main attraction would be the bus out of town."

Chris smiled. They rounded another curve, and suddenly the town was there. The road had become its main street, and on either side of it neat, rectangular buildings squatted in the afternoon sun. Chris quickly spotted three motels with vacancy signs. Spaced between them were other businesses, including some fast-food restaurants. Next to him, he heard Pat give a sigh of relief, but Chris wasn't ready to relax—yet. They had somewhere to eat now, but he wasn't sure that the vacant rooms would be available to a couple of kids.

The bus continued on past the town hall. A sign at the curb said POLICE VEHICLES ONLY, but the two parking spaces were empty. Chris could see the blue water of the gulf behind the buildings lining the left side of the street. One side street dead-ended at a strip of sand where a white lifeguard tower stood silhouetted against the water like a skeleton.

"Westview," the driver said over the speaker system. The bus slowed and pulled up to the curb in front of a T-shirt shop. Other small stores lined both sides of the street for the next few blocks, and Chris quickly scanned the names on the storefronts nearby. He wasn't about to blunder out into the sunlight and be spotted by Clover or Bud before they were there five minutes.

"See anything?" he asked Pat.

"No Cloverbud. No ice cream shop, even. Not right here, anyway."

"Me, neither. Let's go," he said, taking some sunglasses from his pack and slipping them on. Not much of a disguise, but it might help.

Pat put his glasses on, too. They hurried to the front of the bus and stepped out into the afternoon heat, into the inside of a sauna. Chris had seen the ocean, and expected the weather to be cooler here. It wasn't—but he had other things on his mind.

A few people strolled by them while they stood on the sidewalk glancing around, but nobody seemed especially curious. The bus left them in a smelly cloud of exhaust and roared on up the street.

"How far back to the motels?" Pat asked.

"I'd say less than a mile," Chris said, starting in that direction. A whiff of salt air tweaked his nose and he took a deep breath, filling his lungs with it, but it was too warm, too sticky, to be refreshing. He forced it back out through clenched teeth.

"This looks like a pretty nice little town after all," Pat said, falling into step beside him.

"Yeah," Chris said without enthusiasm. He was trying to look at every person walking up and down both sides of the street, without being obvious. The glasses helped.

"I can hardly wait until we leave," Pat said.

**16**

**IN** less than fifteen minutes they were back at the first motel: the Westview Shores. Not new, not fancy, and definitely not on the shore. A quarter mile of side road and several other pieces of property separated it from the beach, but it looked clean.

Chris had a story ready for the desk clerk, an explanation for why he and Pat were staying there by themselves. An aunt and uncle had been delayed in meeting them in town and taking them to their place in the country. Sudden illness—nothing real serious, though. They should be able to get there in a couple of days.

But the woman behind the counter didn't ask. "Thirty-two dollars," was all she said when Chris told her they wanted a room. That was more than Chris had figured this place would cost—quite a bit more—but at least she was willing to take their money, and he doubted that any of the other places would be cheaper. She handed him a registration card. "Payable in advance," she added, and returned her attention to a small television set. The TV blared loudly over the noise of the air conditioner, which didn't seem to be working; the cramped room was hot and stuffy. An orange cat jumped up on the woman's lap, stretched, and plopped down, its eyes on Chris. The woman absentmindedly stroked its chin and chest.

Chris and Pat each put a twenty on the counter. The woman wiped some sweat from the base of her fat neck and made change for them while Chris filled out the registration. "Fred Barnes," he wrote. "Green Bay, Wisconsin." Barely glancing at it, she filed the registration in a drawer under the counter.

"Room eight," she said, handing Chris a key with a green plastic tag attached. The gold number was worn to a shadow. She turned back to the television, her face a mask of indifference.

"Any places around here to get ice cream?" Pat asked.

*Good*, Chris thought. *The direct approach.* Only this woman didn't really seem like the helpful type. She kept staring at the flickering screen. Chris wondered if she'd even heard the question, but then she turned to face Pat.

"Ice cream?" she said, as if waking from a trance.

Chris guessed that they'd just needed to come up with a topic that would get her interested.

"There's the restaurants between here and uptown," she continued. "Did you boys get here on the bus?"

Pat nodded, and Chris let the peculiar sound of her words register. They were different—chewed on and softened and drawn out.

"Then you must've seen some of 'em on the way here from the bus stop. Drive-ins, you know. Handouts, I call 'em. Then there's some more on the other side of the bus stop, in with the shops. Regular restaurants. Some of 'em have milkshakes, sundaes, stuff like that. Good stuff. You might try Murdock's."

Chris watched her swallow. *Her mouth is actually watering*, he thought. "Any shops that just sell ice cream?" he asked. "You know, like ice cream cones and dishes of ice cream?"

"Not yet," she said dreamily, a little grin lifting up the corners of her mouth. "But there's one opening up soon, I hear." The word "hear" came out "he-uh."

"When? Where?" Chris asked, hoping he didn't sound anxious.

She didn't seem to notice. "A few more days, I think, probably after you boys leave. How long are you staying, anyway?"

"Just a couple of days," Chris said. "Until my aunt and uncle get here." At least he'd gotten to use part of his story.

"Where?" Pat said.

The woman looked at him with a blank expression.

"Where...is...the...ice...cream...shop?" he asked slowly, dragging out each word.

Chris could see him losing his patience.

"It ain't open yet," she said.

Pat looked over at Chris for some help.

"Can you tell us where it *will* be when it opens?" Chris asked. "Just in case we're still here?"

"Sure," she said, as if wondering why they hadn't asked earlier. "It's about two blocks past the bus stop—the T-shirt shop—but on the water side of the street. The same side as the post office and Murdock's. Next to the toy shop—you can't miss it. The name's already up. Kinda cute," she said, looking past Chris at the window behind him, as if the name were painted there. "The Cloverbud," she said, but it came out "Cuhlovuhbud." She shook her head slowly. "Not sure what it has to do with ice cream, but it's kinda pretty."

Chris had stopped listening to her after "Cloverbud." Having her say the name triggered an instant replay of everything that had happened in the last few days. The knot in his stomach tightened, and he could feel the sweat forming in his pores. He glanced at Pat, who looked nervous and excited at the same time. "Let's go, Rocky," he said.

"Thanks," Pat said to the woman.

They were halfway across the office when she yelled, "Hey!"

Chris froze, then cautiously turned around, watching Pat do the same. The woman looked at them without blinking, her eyes glistening in the sunlight coming in through the half-open window blinds. Then a faint grin lifted the corners of her mouth. "Go, Packers!" she shouted, smiling broadly and raising her fist in the air. Chris watched cat hairs drop from her hand and drift slowly down in the dusty light, while his heartbeat gradually returned to normal.

"Go, Packers," Pat said, forcing a smile.

Chris couldn't even do that. "Yeah," he said, and turned back for the door.

They found their room easily. With three others, it formed the bottom of the motel's "U" shape, its window and door facing the street. A small swimming pool surrounded by short green shrubbery and white gravel took up most of the courtyard in front of it.

Inside, the room was dark and hot and smelled faintly of mildew and pesticide. Pat turned on the air conditioning unit under the window while Chris opened the drapes and looked around. On the wall to his left, a low dresser supported a lamp and television. On the opposite wall, two double beds were separated by a nightstand, table lamp, and phone. Doors opened to a closet and bathroom at the far end of the small room.

They dropped their backpacks on the little circular table near the window and sat down in two straight-backed chairs. Outside, the sun had dropped low enough behind the motel that half of the courtyard was shaded. Chris looked at his watch— 6:05. At home it was 5:05. Their parents wouldn't be missing them yet. His mom was usually the first one home, at about five-thirty. In a half-hour she'd be reading the note. Pat's parents would find theirs about fifteen minutes later, but Chris suspected that his mom would be waiting for Pat's parents with some bad news when they got home.

"So far, so good," Pat said.

"We're here, anyway," Chris said.

"And we already know where the shop is," said Pat. "Now to find the house."

"The sooner the better." He realized that now he was ready to get this over with, one way or another. He walked to the phone, got an outside line, and dialed information. The number the operator gave him matched the one they already had. When he asked for the address she referred him to another number, which he wrote down on the small pad of paper on the nightstand and quickly dialed. He asked for the address to be repeated twice, carefully writing it on the notepad.

"Four-seventeen East Orchard," he said, hanging up the phone. "Now all we have to—"

"Chris!" Pat shouted, his nose pressed to the window.

Chris started toward him and then stalled halfway there, unable to move. Lumbering out of the bend in the highway and heading for town on the straight section of road in front of the motel was a big white van with a giant ice cream cone painted on the side. Chris didn't have to read the words below it. He knew what they said.

Sunlight glinting off the driver's window made it difficult to see who was behind the wheel. But Chris picked out the shape of his head—big and blocky, like the rest of him.

"It's Bud!" Pat said, his voice now a fierce whisper.

The van disappeared, cut off from view by the front of the motel.

"Come on!" Chris said, yanking open the door. In a moment they were carefully peering around the wall of the motel office, down the road toward town, watching the white van get smaller in the distance, watching it slow, its right turn signal flashing. Watching it turn a quarter mile away and head east, disappearing from view once more.

"He didn't go to the shop," Chris said. "It's farther down on the other side of the street."

"The house?" Pat wondered out loud.

"Could be," Chris said, grabbing Pat by the shirt sleeve and starting back toward the room. His heart was thumping in his chest, and it wasn't from the short sprint to the front of the courtyard. "Or maybe he's already making his ice cream rounds in the neighborhoods."

"It looked like he was heading somewhere definite," Pat said.

"I hope you're right," Chris said. "Let's find out."

They headed for town, stopping at a gas station a block away, where the attendant confirmed that Orchard Street was three more blocks straight ahead. And the East Orchard address would be reached by turning right off the main road, which he called Palm Avenue. They each got a can of soda pop from an old machine in front of the station and continued toward town.

They turned right on Orchard and walked a nervous first block. The neighborhood of small frame houses was quiet. Two small boys were playing in the dirt in front of one of the houses; they didn't even look up. There were no adults in sight and no cars traveling the narrow street.

"Get ready to run for it or hide behind something if anyone comes," Chris said. He knew the sunglasses wouldn't save them if Bud or Clover were suddenly to drive down the street.

"What kind of car do they have?" Pat asked as they crossed the street to the next block.

"A big pickup. Green, I think," Chris replied. "With a camper on the back." He could feel sweat trickling down his back. His legs felt heavy and stiff, and he wondered how fast he'd be able to run. There weren't many places to hide. Pat's big body wasn't going to fit behind one of the skinny trees lining the street.

They got past the second block—still no people, no cars on the road. The addresses were in the 200s and getting higher.

The third block was even quieter. The houses were bigger and set back farther from the street. Their numbers were in the 300s. Chris was glad to see more cars parked along the curb here. They'd provide hiding places if necessary.

They came to the end of the block; what Chris saw made the hair on the back of his neck tingle: In the middle of the next block, the big white van sat on the side of the street.

He pushed Pat toward the curb, where an old blue station wagon squatted halfway up on the sidewalk. They ducked down behind it. Chris looked over at Pat, who was blinking the sweat out of his eyes.

"See it?" Chris whispered.

Pat nodded.

Chris glanced around to see if anybody was watching them; they weren't acting exactly normal. But he didn't see anyone. Pat crab-crawled around toward the front of the station wagon, while Chris raised up to get a better look at the ice cream truck. Its back doors were open, and from inside came the sounds of hammering. A shadowy figure was moving around in the dim light of the van's interior.

Pat scrabbled back, a nervous grin on his shiny face. "Bingo," he said.

"Yeah," Chris said. *Now what?* he wondered. They'd accomplished a lot in a short time, but what next? He thought for a moment, listening to his heart race and his stomach churn. "I think we need to come back after dark," he said finally. "We can't get any closer now."

"I was hoping you'd say that. This place is giving me the creeps."

They hurried back up the street, trying to stay low and out of sight, looking over their shoulders to make sure they hadn't been spotted, trying not to appear too suspicious in case people were looking out their front windows. But the hammering from the van continued until it faded to a faint tap-tap-tap in the distance. And no curious faces spied out at them from behind closed draperies. They slowed and walked the rest of the way to Palm Avenue.

"Should we see what's happening at the Cloverbud?" Pat asked when they got back to the main road.

"I guess so," Chris said. "But we need to keep an eye out for Clover. It looks like Bud's going to be busy for a while, but there's no telling where she is."

"My guess is she's in their house somewhere, taking care of a little kid."

"Or a sick mother." But it was good to hear Pat say it. Chris was thinking, hoping the same thing, but he was afraid to say it out loud. For some reason, even though they were in Florida and they'd already found the new Cloverbud and Bud and Clover's house and the ice cream truck, and they'd actually seen Bud, the next step—finding Molly—was still hard to imagine. He had to concentrate on where they were and what they were doing.

Chris looked at his watch—6:45. By now his mom and maybe his dad and probably Pat's parents would know. How was it affecting them? "You think they've called out the National Guard yet?" he asked. "Our parents, I mean?"

"Probably just the FBI," Pat said. He took a deep breath, let it out slowly, and shrugged, as if trying to shed any thoughts of home. "Let's go," he said.

They started toward town, nervously watching the passing cars and pedestrians, checking behind them every few steps to make sure the ice cream truck wasn't back on the road. Chris felt as if they were walking down the middle of the street carrying neon signs that said RUNAWAY.

They passed two drive-in restaurants. The smells of hamburgers and french fries drifted out to the sidewalk, reminding Chris of how hungry he was. He could imagine what Pat was thinking about, but didn't ask. Not yet. He just had to get to The Cloverbud.

The T-shirt shop was closed when they walked past it. They crossed the street and continued north past other shops, some of which were still open. At Murdock's they paused. The aroma of cooking coming out the open door of the little restaurant was overwhelming and stopped them in their tracks. They looked at the menu posted by the door and stared in through the big front window. The place was crowded. People sharing a meal, couples and families, talking and laughing. Suddenly Chris wanted to see his family—all of them.

"On the way back," Pat said, pulling him away from the window. "Let's eat here on the way back."

The Cloverbud was on the next block. They approached it cautiously, but it was empty and locked. From the outside it looked much like the original Cloverbud except for the signs of ongoing remodeling. Boards and sawhorses and tools and a ladder were visible through the front window. Debris was scattered around on the wood floor.

But it looked mostly complete. Cabinets and a big sign listing the varieties of ice cream were hung on the far wall. Everything was freshly painted, and stretching across the back of the room was a large freezer display case and counter.

They peered into the dim interior of the shop, looking for something, some sign that things weren't quite right here: a piece of child's clothing, a toy, a doll. But would they have even brought her down here? Chris didn't think so.

"I don't see anything weird," Pat said.

Chris looked up and down the street, checking the cars and pedestrians. "Me, neither," he said. "I think we need to look around back."

A narrow sidewalk between shops led them to an alley that ran behind all the buildings on the west side of Palm. There was nothing but more building scraps and garbage in back of The Cloverbud. The door was locked.

They got back to the street just as a dark blue police car cruised slowly by. The driver's head turned mechanically from side to side, as if he were looking for something—or some*one*. He glanced in their direction, and then—without missing a beat—away, toward the other side of the street. Chris wondered if this was just a routine patrol for this guy. Probably, he decided, but his skin felt crawly under the layer of sweat.

"Don't look," Pat said, heading up the sidewalk with Chris at his side.

Chris didn't look. He pretended to be interested in the shops as they walked past, gazing into the windows of The Cloverbud and then of a toy store next to it. Finally, out of the corner of his eye, he saw the cruiser pick up speed. He watched it continue on down the street. "Phew!" he said, breathing again. "I wonder what he was so interested in."

"You," Pat said. "It's your criminal appearance. It's bound to make people suspicious."

"Ha, ha," Chris said. "Very funny."

**17**

**A** young blond woman met them inside the door of Murdock's and showed them to a corner table. The smell of food and the sounds of the people around them talking and eating made Chris suddenly feel comfortable. For a moment he stopped thinking about the reason they were sitting there.

But then just as quickly he remembered. From his seat, he could look through the front window out to the street. Fifty feet past the restaurant, the police car, empty now, was parked at the curb. Where was the policeman?

Pat, his back to the window, must have seen the change in his expression. "What's the matter, Chris?" he asked.

Instead of answering, Chris swivelled his head

slowly to the right. Directly across from them, against the opposite wall, the policeman sat at a small table by himself, looking at a menu.

"The Westview police force is here," Chris said, his voice low and scratchy. "But don't gawk at him. Just act natural." Easy to say, but Chris was having a hard time acting natural himself.

A waitress brought them menus, and Chris watched Pat's eyes drift off the page and over toward the other corner. "Real subtle, Rocky," Chris whispered. "Why don't you just read the menu so we can eat and get out of here."

"He's looking this way," Pat said, his voice a hoarse whisper, his lips barely moving.

Chris stared down at the menu, but the words were a blur. "Just don't be strange," he said.

"Maybe we should take off these glasses," Pat said.

Chris looked at Pat and knew he was right. What normal people wore sunglasses inside a restaurant? They wouldn't have looked much more bizarre if they'd been wearing funny noses and hats with propellers on top. He took his glasses off as casually as he could, and Pat did, too. They both studied their menus furiously, not looking right or left.

Chris had just begun actually focusing in on the words when a shadow fell over the table. The waitress, he hoped. No, not the waitress—a man. A tall man with a gray uniform and a gun and a badge and a name plate that said "Hudson." And topping it all was a young face and old hair—nearly white. The man was smiling, but Chris had seen that smile before. His football coach wore that smile whenever he was getting ready to make them do push-ups.

"You boys on your own tonight?" he asked, his smile fading out and then coming back.

"Yeah," Pat said, as if that were the most natural situation in the world.

*Don't overdo it,* Chris thought.

"On vacation?" Hudson said.

"Visiting relatives," Chris said. His heart was trying to crawl into his stomach.

"In town here?"

Chris could feel Hudson's eyes homing in on him, looking for a little crack, a chink in the armor.

"No. Out in the country. My aunt and uncle. They're picking us up here." *Go away,* Chris thought. *Go away and let us alone. Go find some real criminals.*

"Sounds like fun," Hudson said, but his expression didn't look like he expected them to have any. "City boys, I take it?"

*City boys.* Chris didn't like the way he said it—down-home soft and friendly, but with a hard, inhospitable edge. He could imagine him saying "drug dealers" the same way. And what city? What story should they tell him? Were they still Rocky and

Fred from Green Bay?

"Yeah, we're from the city," Pat said, and Hudson's stare shifted back across the table.

Out of the corner of his eye, Chris saw a figure glide up and stop beside the policeman. The waitress—at last. Maybe if she broke the bulldog's concentration, he'd drop his bone and go back to his corner.

"You gonna let these boys read their menus this evenin', Roy?" she said, resting a hand on Hudson's arm. "They look pretty hungry to me." Her "pretty" came out "purty"—a sweet, comfortable word.

Hudson looked at her, a narrow-eyed glare at first, but then his expression softened as she returned his look with a smile—the biggest, prettiest smile Chris had ever seen. "Sure, Katie," he said. "They can read their menus. We were just having a little visit."

"That's good, big fella," she said, straightening his badge. "Now why don't you go over and sit down, put up your feet and pick out some supper, and I'll be right over to take care of you."

"Sounds good," Hudson said, taking his eyes off Katie long enough to glance back at Chris and Pat. "Nice talking to you, boys," he said. "Hope you have a good time here." It sounded more like an order than a hope. "See you in a minute, Katie," he said with a smile—a real smile, Chris thought, surprised that he had one. Hudson walked back to his table, unhurriedly surveying the restaurant before he sat down.

"That boy needs to take a break," Katie said, loud enough for Hudson to hear. "He sees an outlaw behind every bush." She smiled that big smile again, looking first at Chris and then at Pat. "Sorry he was givin' you all a hard time in here."

"No problem," Pat said, puffing out his chest, trying to act nonchalant, unconcerned. Chris figured Pat was about one smile away from falling in love.

"You ready to order?" she asked, turning to Chris. He decided he got preference because Pat was obviously too sophisticated to be hungry.

But after Chris chose a dinner, so did Pat, and Katie hurried off for Hudson's table. They both managed to avoid letting their eyes wander in that direction. Instead, they shared a quick look of relief, and pretended to study the tabletop, where a cartoon map of Florida showing all the major tourist attractions was sandwiched between the table and a clear slab of plastic. Westview wasn't on the map.

Chris couldn't believe how fortunate they'd been that Katie had come along when she had. He didn't know how much longer they would have been able to make their story work; it had a lot of holes in it, if someone decided to look a little closer. And Chris was sure that Hudson was capable of looking more than a little closer. But Katie—she'd done a lot more than just break his concentration. She'd blown it apart and sent him on his way, thinking about something completely different. Chris hoped Hudson would stay distracted the rest of the night; he didn't want to face that icy smile again.

Katie brought the policeman's meal first—*on purpose?* Chris wondered—and Hudson was nearly finished by the time she carried theirs from the kitchen. They'd just started eating when he got up, said something to Katie that made her laugh, and headed for the door. Chris chanced a look in his direction, forcing a smile, and got a nod in return. Pat was concentrating on his food—or pretending to.

Chris was full when Katie came back to the table, and Pat was just picking at what was left of his food—a small mound of some kind of vegetable that Chris didn't recognize. His mound was still sitting intact on his plate.

"Dessert, fellas?" she said.

Chris looked out the window. It wasn't quite dark. They had a little while longer to stall.

"We've got some homemade key lime pie," she said, smiling, glancing back and forth between Pat and Chris.

"I'll have some," Chris said, although he wasn't sure what key lime pie was. He liked lemon; maybe this was something similar.

"Me, too," Pat said, looking up at her dreamily.

She brought the pie, and it *was* good. By the time they finished it, it was dark. They left her a tip on the table—a good one, but not *too* good; they didn't want to appear overly grateful for what she'd done, or jump to the front of her mind if somebody should come around asking about them. And they were starting to realize how much things cost—and how quickly their money would dwindle if they had to stay here very long. They paid their bill, thanked her, and walked out the door into the night.

Chris had expected that with the dark, the weather would cool off, but it hadn't. The same blast of hot, wet air hit them as they left the air-conditioned restaurant. The only thing missing was the sunshine. He glanced at his watch—almost nine o'clock. "Should we do it?" he said, trying to sound brave, but he'd had to force himself to think of Molly—of what they were trying to accomplish—before the words would even come out.

"Yeah," Pat said. "Let's see what's going on." They started walking, heading south, past small, slow-moving knots of people, and cramped, cluttered shops getting ready to close their doors. The little town was pulling in its sidewalks for the night.

As they got farther away from Murdock's and closer to Orchard Street, Chris felt a weight descending on him in the darkness. Pat had grown quiet, nearly silent. Chris thought that Pat must be feeling the same burden.

They crossed Palm and started down Orchard, heading east. The neighborhood had changed in just a few hours. It was dark now, gloomy. The few street lights cast dark shadows near houses. Some houses were lit only by the dim lamps from shaded interiors, and here and there a yellow porch light. It was quiet, the only sounds coming from traffic passing behind them on Palm, and that was infrequent and fading as they got farther away.

"This place is spooky," Pat said after they'd walked the first block in silence. A dog barked in a yard across the street. A big, ugly bark. They involuntarily picked up their pace.

"Just pretend it's a bad dream," Chris said. It felt like that to him—somebody else's nightmare.

"When do we wake up?" Pat asked.

Chris didn't answer. He didn't know. Soon, he hoped.

They slowed as they approached Bud and Clover's house. It was brightly lit inside, but the curtains and drapes were drawn in every window, allowing only soft, narrow rays of light to escape to the front lawn and shrubs. The backyard was surrounded by a six-foot-tall wooden fence that separated it from the front yard and the neighboring lot, where a similar house sat.

When they reached the edge of the yard, they

stopped. The big white van sat in the driveway on the other side of the house, closed up, dark, and quiet. The top of its ice cream cone rose like a chocolate moon above the pickup truck and camper parked next to it. The light from the house's side windows reflected off the pickup's shiny green paint and the camper's white metal. The night was still warm but Chris felt a chill.

"Looks like they're both home," Pat whispered.

"I think you're right," Chris whispered. *I hope all three of them are home,* he thought.

"What do you want to do?" Pat asked.

Chris thought for a moment, his eyes darting around the yard. "Let's see what the back looks like," he said.

They stepped into the neighbor's yard and crept along the white picket fence marking the property line. They reached the tall wooden fence, followed it to its end, and turned left along the rear boundary of Bud and Clover's yard. Midway down the back section of fence they stopped. Dim light from the house filtered through a knothole halfway up one of the vertical boards.

Chris stooped down to look, but his nose brushed the rough, bare wood before his eye got to the hole. He stopped, breathing in. It was moist and smelled freshly cut—new. Why would they put up a new fence, unless they were trying to keep someone out—

or in? Or maybe for privacy. He glanced over his shoulder at the land behind him. In the darkness he could see that they were standing on a narrow dirt alleyway. Beyond that there was nothing but a vacant lot. He could make out the shapes of bushes and trees, and the smell of rotting vegetation filled his nose. No need for privacy here, unless Clover and Bud had something to hide.

Pat crouched down next to him. "What do you see?" he said, his voice barely audible.

"Nothing yet," Chris whispered. "But the fence is new, Pat. The fence is *new.*"

Pat ran his fingers over the boards and nudged Chris out of the way, sticking his face up to the knothole. "I've been eating my carrots," he said. "Let me take a look." He knelt there for a moment, motionless. "I wonder what—" he began. Then, in an excited whisper, "Look in here, Chris! Tell me what you see."

Chris shifted back over and peered through the hole, his heart racing. But at first he saw nothing out of the ordinary, just the back of the house, and silhouetted against the light from the windows and door, a clothesline. Then he saw another kind of framework, off to the side of the clothesline, resting on the lawn like a dinosaur skeleton. His heart accelerated, fluttering in his chest now, and he took a deep breath of rancid air.

"A swing set," he whispered, and let out his

breath in a low whistle.

"And I don't think it's for little Buddy Boy," Pat said.

*No,* Chris thought. *And not for Clover, either.* For a split second he wondered if it had been left by the previous owners. But he chose not to think so. Bud and Clover would've told them they didn't want it, or hauled it away by now.

For the next hour they slapped at mosquitoes and took turns looking through the fence. They watched the lights go out one by one, until the house was dark except for a faint glow seeping from one back window.

"A night light?" Pat asked.

"Molly doesn't like the dark," Chris said, remembering a little lamp shaped like a tugboat that had to be turned on when she went to bed.

Several minutes passed, slowly and uneventfully. Chris wasn't sure what to do next.

"I've been thinking," Pat said.

"Uh, oh," Chris said.

Pat ignored the sarcasm. "I think we need to come back tomorrow morning," he said, "and wait for Bud to leave. I think we can handle Clover."

Chris thought about the idea. He hated to leave, now that they were so close. But he didn't see how they'd be able to break into the house in the dark, find Molly, and get out without waking Bud and

Clover. And they weren't doing any good out here behind the fence.

Something moved in the bushes behind them—some kind of animal.

"Okay," Chris said, "but we need to get back here early. Before daylight."

They decided to take the alley instead of cutting through the neighbor's yard again. It led them to Fourth Street, where they took a left, and then a right on the next block. In five minutes they were back on Palm, heading toward the motel.

There was little traffic on the street, and most of the businesses had closed down for the night. Chris and Pat walked along quietly, their thoughts somewhere else. Chris found himself barely able to think. He felt like a little kid on the night before Christmas. The anticipation was charging him up, causing his mind to spin. But he was trying to come up with some ideas, some kind of plan for tomorrow morning. So he didn't notice the car slide up to the curb.

"Hey, guys!" The voice was young, friendly. The words came out "Hey, gazz!" Chris and Pat turned toward the car at the same time, stopping in the middle of the sidewalk. Less than a block away, the lights from their motel shone out onto the street.

A kid with short blond hair was leaning out the front passenger window of a shiny black car. It sat low to the ground, distant thunder coming from the exhaust. Chris studied his face: smiling mouth, cold eyes. He had an urge to grab Pat and run, but curiosity held him in check. And something else— something hypnotic.

The driver and another passenger in the back seat made it a trio leering out at them from the inside of the car. The one in the back seat rolled down his window—another grinning face with short dark hair, chewing gum furiously.

"You guys got ten dollars you can loan us for gas?" the blond said, still smiling.

Chris reached for his wallet and stopped. Pat had a dead man's grip on his elbow.

"We don't have any money," Pat said. His voice had an edge on it that Chris had heard only a few other times.

"Yeah?" the gum chewer said. "Your little friend thinks he does."

"He doesn't," Pat said.

Chris looked at Pat's face. His eyes had narrowed and his jaw jutted out, silhouetted against the soft, yellow glow of a nearby street lamp.

"Let's go, Pat," Chris said softly.

Pat ignored him.

"I don't believe you, *boy*," the blond said, his smile faded to a smirk. "We're gonna have to come and see for ourselves."

The engine's rumble was deep, loud, but Chris's

heartbeat was louder. He wanted to be somewhere else, anywhere else, but Pat was standing his ground.

"You best not get out, *boy*," Pat said, and took a step toward the car.

Chris couldn't believe it. Pat actually took a step *toward the car.* What was he doing? These guys had to be at least sixteen. They were riding around in a car, and they looked big. Boys in men's bodies—and there were three of them.

But for some reason they didn't get out. The blond had opened his door a couple of inches, but he just sat there, his expression a contorted combination of surprise and anger. And something else—disbelief? Fear? Chris tugged on Pat's shirtsleeve.

"Let's go, Pat," he repeated.

Pat stood his ground.

"You a tough guy?" the blond asked, coating his words with sarcasm.

Pat answered them with a glare, his fists clenched into white-knuckled balls.

"Your little friend a tough guy, too?" the gum chewer smacked from the back seat.

Chris watched the driver lean forward to get a better view. His face was in the dark, but Chris could see a grin. He could hear him giggling softly, nervously.

"You don't want to find out how tough either of us is," Pat said defiantly. His voice sounded confident, old. And lower. Like a bullfrog's call in the night—a big bullfrog.

For a long moment it was a standoff. Chris and Pat stood motionless on the sidewalk. The three nightriders stared out at them from the car without moving, their faces disfigured by shadows and murky light. Chris could feel his fight-or-flight juices flowing. *Fly,* they were telling him. But he knew what Pat's were saying, and Chris wasn't going to leave him there. Chris was aware of lights—a car—coming up the street from his left, but his eyes were on the car in front of him—and the guys inside it.

The door opened on the other side, then the passenger's door opened. The driver and the blond eased out of the car and stood there, waiting for the gum chewer to follow.

Suddenly they were bathed in blue and red lights, flashing, bouncing off the car's shiny chrome and paint and lighting up the faces of the two bullies as they glanced quickly behind them, snaked back into the car, and closed the doors.

A police car coasted silently to a stop three feet behind the rear bumper of the black car. Its radio barked into the still night as the driver's door opened and Hudson unfolded his long frame from the seat. His smile was back, the bulldog smile. But Chris was glad to see it. This time it was directed at someone else.

Hudson ignored the driver and walked to the passenger side, stopping and glaring at the blond kid in the front seat. "What are you squirrels up to, C.J.?" he asked, his voice soft but demanding.

"Nothing," the kid said. "Just driving around, Officer Hudson."

"Is that right, boys?" he asked, glancing in Pat and Chris's direction before refocusing his icy stare on C.J.'s face.

Chris was about to say yes, that was right. After all, these guys weren't going to bother them now. *Just send them on their way, Officer Hudson,* he thought.

"They wanted us to *loan* them ten dollars," Pat said.

The gum chewer gave Pat a look that made Chris's heart skip, but Pat glared right back at him.

"Just for gas," C.J. said. "We just needed some gas money."

"Turn your instrument lights on, Wayne," Hudson said, bending over to look at the driver. The dashboard lit up, and the upper half of the policeman's body disappeared into the passenger compartment as he leaned through the open window. The handle of his pistol stuck out at an angle from his belt. He straightened up to his full height and let his gaze flit back and forth between C.J. and the kid in the back. Chris watched them shrink down in their seats.

"Appears to me you boys got pretty near a full tank of gas," Hudson said.

No answer.

"You shakin' these young guys down?"

No answer.

"You know, I can think of a couple of reasons to lock you boys up right now," Hudson said.

"Lock us up?" C.J. said. "What for?"

"How about attempted robbery and assault, to start with?"

"We weren't really gonna do nothin'," C.J. said, his voice becoming a whine.

"Is that why you were getting out of the car?" Chris asked. He was beginning to enjoy this.

C.J. didn't answer. Instead, he began drumming his fingers on the dashboard.

"I'll tell you what," Hudson said, bending down again. The smile was gone from his face. "I'll follow you on home, Wayne, and you be sure to drive real careful because I'm gonna be looking for any kind of infraction. Then we're gonna ask your folks to call up C.J.'s and Marty's folks and invite 'em over. And I'm gonna call up old Raymond and ask him to come over, too. I think your football coach should be there, don't you? Then we'll all sit down and have ourselves a little court session."

He stood back up, raising his voice above the throb of the engine. "When I honk, you can start for home, Wayne. If you think you can make three miles on a tank of gas, that is."

The smile was back when he turned and started for his car. As he opened his door he paused and looked over at Chris and Pat. "You boys better hurry to wherever you're going," he said. "There's much worse than these three punks out on the road at night, and I can't be everywhere at once."

"We will, Officer Hudson," Chris said. Suddenly all he wanted was to be back in the motel room. He glanced at the three kids, but the tinted car windows were rolled up, obscuring their faces.

The blue-and-red flashers stopped, the horn honked, and both cars pulled slowly away from the curb, heading out of town. Chris looked over at Pat, who was smiling broadly.

"Fun, huh?" Pat said.

Chris just shook his head. "Let's go," he said, and started for the motel.

Pat caught up with him. "Well, you have to admit that it took your mind off things, didn't it?"

"I could fall asleep to take my mind off things," Chris said, "and not be in danger of getting killed."

"They wouldn't have killed us. Just beaten us up and taken our money. And we might've gotten some punches in ourselves. I think I could've taken that blond guy."

"That would've only left two for me. You're such a

comfort, Pat."

"They made me mad."

"Well, try not to let it affect your judgment next time. We've got some serious business coming up."

"Yeah," Pat said. "Okay." His head was down, his eyes on the sidewalk.

"But thanks for being a tough guy," Chris said. He didn't want Pat to think he wasn't appreciated. "You had them thinking. They almost didn't get out of the car."

"Almost," Pat said, and then he laughed, low and quiet at first, and then high-pitched and loud. And suddenly Chris was laughing with him, nervous energy pouring out into the sticky night air.

Fifteen minutes later they were in their beds. Chris lay in the dark motel room wondering if he'd be able to sleep. His body was exhausted, running on empty, but his mind was racing. So much had happened in one day that it seemed as if he'd been up for a week. Had it really been just that morning that they'd left home? What were his mom and dad going through now? And what would happen tomorrow?

He listened to Pat's long, deep breaths and soft snoring, and wondered how he could fall asleep so easily. But five minutes later he closed his eyes himself, drifting effortlessly into sleep's whirlpool.

**THE** cry of a siren floated through Chris's dream. On the TV screen were crowds of civilians and soldiers and police. Fighting, battling in the streets of some far-off city, on a continent where the most terrifying beasts in the jungle now carried clubs and wore uniforms and masks of hatred.

He was sitting in the big stuffed chair with his grandmother, and the scene played before them on the old console television in her living room. But he knew it wasn't just a movie. He was only a little kid, but he knew it was real. He could tell by the look on his grandmother's face and the way she shook her head. And then she had said it—a quote from the Bible that he would hear her utter often over the years to come. "For they have sown the wind, and they shall reap the whirlwind."

The wail of the siren became the screech of the alarm clock, and he woke up. He sat upright and swung his feet to the floor, fumbling in the dark for the clock radio. He switched off the alarm. His grandmother's words hung in the air like a rain cloud, weighing on his senses, dampening his hopes.

What had he sown? And what was he now going to reap?

Pat was sitting up in bed. Chris could make out his shape in the dim light filtering in from the street lamps. And he was saying something.

"What?" Chris said.

"You didn't hear me?" Pat said. "Where were you, dreamland?"

"Something like that."

"I said, are you ready to go get your little sister?"

Chris was surprised to find that he *was* ready. Despite the dream and what it had done to his spirits just a moment earlier, he was ready. Maybe Bud and Clover would reap the whirlwind. "I'm way past ready," he said.

Twenty minutes later they were squatting behind Bud and Clover's back fence. They'd made their way down the streets and back alley without seeing anyone. Most of the houses, including Bud and Clover's, were still dark inside. Off to their right, dawn was creeping into the eastern sky. Chris peered at his watch—5:30.

He looked through the knothole, checking for something—anything—they might have missed last night, but the yard looked the same. He sat down on the ground next to Pat and waited.

At six o'clock, a light came on in a back room. The other bedroom, Chris figured. At least they were up. Now, how much longer until Bud left?

"What do you think he does all day?" Pat whispered. "Bud, I mean."

"I don't know. Maybe works on getting the shop remodeled. Maybe he's selling ice cream and stuff from the truck already."

"What if he doesn't leave?"

"He'll leave," Chris said. "He has to."

They waited. Daylight came and the sun rose through the trees, painting shadows on the fence. Chris and Pat no longer had the darkness to hide them, but at least there was no one else around. The big vacant lot behind them was thick with pines and saplings and undergrowth. And only one car had come down the alley; an old lady, looking straight ahead over her steering wheel, was driving it. They pretended to be looking for something in the bushes when she passed, but she didn't even glance at them. They went back to the fence and sat down, and took turns looking through the knothole. And waited.

Finally they heard a door slam shut—a car door,

or maybe a truck. Chris jammed his eye up against the knothole. Across the yard, he could see the upper part of the van over the front section of the backyard fence.

Then a starter cranked and an engine sparked to life. The van engine. It had its own sound and Chris knew it by heart. He glanced at Pat, who'd recognized it, too. Quick smiles lit their faces.

Chris turned back to the hole with Pat hovering next to him, shoulder to shoulder. Then the engine sound changed, and Chris watched the top of the van back away and disappear. "It's moving," he said in a hoarse whisper. "He's leaving." They listened to it stop, shift gears, and accelerate up the street toward Palm. Then the sound was gone.

"How do we know it was Bud driving?" Pat said.

Pat was right, Chris thought. They didn't know. He shrugged his shoulders. "It probably was," he said. But what do they do next? He was sure the doors were locked. And what if Bud were in the house?

"What do you think?" Pat said.

"I don't know," Chris said. "I guess we need to wait. We need to find out who's in the house—look through the windows, maybe. They have to raise those shades sometime, or maybe they'll unlock the door." It sounded good, but how long would they have to wait, and how long would Bud be gone? If it *was*

Bud who had left.

"Maybe it's already unlocked," Pat said. "I could go check."

Chris was thinking about this idea when he heard a click, a bolt being turned in a door. He was sure of it. But locking or unlocking? He didn't know. He looked through the knothole: nothing.

And then suddenly the door swung open. Clover backed out, pushing the screen door open with her wide bottom. She was carrying a plastic laundry basket full of wash. She turned and looked right toward the fence, and for a moment Chris was afraid she'd seen his telltale eye. He jerked back, holding his breath.

"What's going on?" Pat whispered.

"It's Clover," Chris said. "Clover's in the backyard."

"Doing what?"

Chris put his eye back to the hole, and watched her walk over to the clothesline and set the basket on the ground. She reached down, grabbed a blue work shirt, and clothespinned it to the line, obscuring her face and upper body from Chris's view. "She's hanging clothes to dry." He moved out of the way to let Pat take a look.

For Chris's benefit, Pat described in a low whisper what she was hanging up. "Another shirt...a sheet...another sheet...some pants..." Suddenly his whisper rose a notch. *"A dress! A little girl's dress!"* He grabbed Chris by the back of the neck and pulled his face over to the hole. "Look!"

And there it was, little and pink with a white border around the sleeves and collar, hanging from the line. Chris's heart was drumming in his chest and his eyes were watering, blurring his vision. He blinked, and Clover was hanging a shirt. A little red T-shirt with some kind of design on the front.

And then her voice carried across the yard. "Almost done with your cereal, honey?" she called.

Chris couldn't see the back door—the sheets were in the way—but he guessed it was still open. He strained to hear a response from the house. He felt Pat's hand grip his shoulder and tighten, and he thought he heard a voice. Or had he imagined it?

No. "I'll be right there, honey," Clover called. She put a second clothespin on the shirt and headed for the back door, disappearing behind the sheets.

"Should we go for it?" Pat asked. He'd maneuvered Chris out of the way so he could look again.

"I don't know," Chris said. He wanted to, he wanted to badly, but was this the time? They still hadn't seen her. He pushed Pat aside again and peered through the hole: nothing yet. And where was Bud? How long until he got back? Chris decided it was time to do it.

But then Clover's voice carried back to them, getting louder as she moved from the house to the yard. "You can just bring your little chair and your dolly out here, honey, and watch me hang the clothes," she said. Her feet appeared below the bottom of the sheets. Next to her, the legs of a little wooden chair hung above the ground before settling into the grass. Then the lower halves of two little bare legs materialized. And feet, in red tennis shoes—shoes Chris didn't recognize. But so what? They could have gotten new shoes for her.

A baby doll with tousled blond hair dropped to the ground next to the chair. Chris caught a glimpse of a tiny hand as it reached down to retrieve the doll and lift it out of his sight. He held his breath, his heart hammering in his throat.

"What's going on?" Pat whispered.

Chris wasn't sure he could talk without shouting, but he managed a raspy whisper. "She's in the yard. Molly's in the yard, but I can't see her face—she's behind the sheets."

Pat moved him gently out of the way and pressed his face to the fence. "Just her legs," he said after a moment. "But I think that's enough. Let's get her."

Chris didn't answer. He was trying to decide if they could get over the fence and across the yard before Clover could grab Molly and get into the house. He moved Pat out of the way again. He wanted another look. "Let me see something first," he said, ignoring Pat's impatient glance.

He stared through the hole, calculating the distance to the clothesline, and between Clover and the back door. Could they do it?

A strong breeze suddenly swept across the backyard, pushing the sheet bottoms up to the level of Clover's knees. And Molly's stomach. Chris's heart skipped. *A little higher. Just a little higher*, he thought. But the breeze died and he was back to looking at ankles and feet. Then another sudden gust. The sheets flapped up for a split second. High. High enough.

And he couldn't believe what he'd seen. Just a glimpse, but it was enough.

He pushed himself away from the fence and sat down with his head in his hands, staring at the ground. After all this! He'd just lost Molly, again.

"What's the matter?" Pat said.

"It's not her, Pat," Chris said, trying to swallow the lump in his throat. "It's not her."

"What?" Pat said, pressing his eye to the hole. "How do you know?"

"I saw her, I saw her hair—short. No, not just short—dark, real dark."

Pat turned and sat next to him, letting out a long breath. For a minute he said nothing. Then: "I was sure she was here! Who *is* that little girl, anyway?"

CHRIS thought. He thought hard. Something was still letting a little beam of light in. Where was it coming from? Then he heard a sound.

"Shhh!" Chris said, his finger to his lips, his heart back in his throat. Together he and Pat listened to the little girl recite a poem to her doll.

> My little girl with golden hair,
> Awakes to find me standing there,
> A bit of sleep still in her eyes,
> My little girl, my sweet surprise.

Pat smiled over at him. A big smile—a huge smile. And Chris returned it, tears pooling up in the corners of his eyes.

"Can you handle Clover?" Chris said. "Long enough for me to get Molly over to the gate, anyway?"

Pat gave Chris his "No problem" look, though it wasn't quite convincing. "A fat, fifty-year-old woman?" he said. "I think so. For a while, anyway. And then what?"

"Head for town," Chris said. "If Hudson or somebody else isn't at the police station, we'll go to Murdock's, or someplace else where there's people. Someone will help us."

"Okay," Pat said. They stood and faced the fence.

"Now!" Chris said.

In an instant they'd scrambled up the side of the rough wooden fence and leaped over, landing on the soft ground at the same time. Clover had moved from behind the sheets and was bending over the basket, reaching for another piece of laundry. She didn't hear them, didn't see them at first. They were halfway across the yard, running, when she sensed something and looked up. She stood, the expression on her round face changing quickly from confusion to recognition to shock to horror.

"What?" she said. The word was a squeak. "How?" Her mouth formed the word and stayed open in a dark oval of fear. She turned toward the house just as they reached the clothesline. Pat grabbed her from behind, pinning her arms to her sides.

"No-oh-oh-oh!" The word came out in a long, throbbing sob, filling the air, and she struggled to get free.

Chris cut left through the hanging clothes, and suddenly she was there, staring at Pat and Clover's awkward dance, watching them tumble to the ground in a squirming heap. She looked up at Chris from her little chair and he knew it was her. He knew it was Molly.

A big smile suddenly pushed away the confusion on her face. "Kis!" she squealed, and he swept her up in his arms, pivoting toward the gate, sprinting past Pat and Clover silently wrestling on the ground. "Patty!" she called down to him, squeezing Chris's neck.

"I'll...be...right...there...Molly," Pat said to her. The words popped out in short grunts.

They reached the gate. Padlocked! A big, heavy padlock hung through the latch. Without hesitating, Chris boosted Molly over the top of the fence, prying her little fingers from his neck and squeezing them onto the fencetop, hanging her over the other side.

"Hang on for a second, Molly," he said, and pulled himself to the top and over, landing on the packed gravel of the driveway in front of the green pickup. He lowered her to the ground, holding her close to his leg. "Pat!" he yelled. "Let's go!"

In a twinkling, Pat was on top of the fence. He looked back once and dropped to the ground next to Chris, breathing hard. "She's heading for the house— the phone—let's get out of here!" Molly looked up at him, her eyes wide. "I'll carry Molly for a while," he said. "We can go faster."

Chris didn't argue; Pat was right.

Pat scooped her up and she held on, her arms and legs wrapped around him. He sprinted down the driveway and turned left, pressing Molly to his chest with his right arm. Chris kept pace next to him.

Side by side they raced down the sidewalks of Orchard Street, heading for Palm. They covered the first block. And the second. And the third. Then Chris looked up. A block away, a big white van was turning left from Palm to Orchard, its tires squealing, its body leaning as it careened toward them.

"Bud!" Chris gasped. "C'mon!" They veered right, cutting across Orchard at the intersection, heading north on First. Pat was slowing down. Chris could hear him straining for air.

"Let me take her now," Chris said, and they slowed to a jog, exchanging Molly like a bundle of fragile cargo. Pat was having trouble catching his breath.

When they raced off again, Chris glanced over his shoulder. Less than a half block away, Bud was plowing through a left turn from Orchard onto First. He'd seen them. Chris could hear the scream of the tires and brakes.

"He's coming!" he yelled. Molly tightened her grip around the back of his neck. He felt her heart beating against his chest. Her breath was coming in little sobs. And his lungs were burning, aching. What could they do now?

"We need to get off the street!" Pat gasped. "The next house! Cut through the yard!"

Chris could hear the roar of the truck behind them now, louder and louder. They reached a hedge and veered left from the sidewalk onto the grass, sprinting for the backyard, and another house beyond that, and Palm somewhere in the distance. His legs were cement, but Molly was a feather in his arms, as if she were part of him.

The sound of skidding tires filled the air. Close, too close, but Chris didn't look back. Pat's hand was on his elbow, urging him ahead. And they were flying now, racing down a narrow corridor between houses, looking for the best—the fastest—escape route. They had to get back to the business area, where there were people—where somebody would help them.

They pushed through a low gate into a fenced backyard, and Pat steered Chris toward the far corner, where the fence had rotted and sagged over. From far behind them, Chris heard a voice carrying through the hot, sticky air—air that was clogging his lungs, making him gasp for breath. It was Bud's voice, but different than Chris remembered it. Chris heard anger in it now, and urgency and hurt.

"Molly!" he shouted. "Don't let them take you,

Molly! We love you! Aunt Clover loves you!"

Molly held on tighter, pressing her face against Chris's collarbone, and he accelerated, tapping an extra reserve of energy he didn't know was there.

"Chris!" the voice called, growing fainter. "Don't run! Come back!" Then an instant later: "We can talk!"

But Chris didn't want to talk. He wanted to run; he wanted to *fly*. They reached the broken-down fence, and Pat leaped up on it, his weight flattening it down, closer to the ground—close enough that Chris could run up and over it without breaking stride, without slowing down. He was in another yard now, still heading west, and he glanced back to make sure Pat was coming.

He saw Pat, a few strides back and gaining, and beyond Pat, through the gap between two houses, he saw something else: a flash of white on the street, heading north. "The truck's going up First," he wheezed, as Pat drew even with him. "Bud's trying to cut us off."

"We'll have to get around him," Pat said, grabbing Chris's arm, urging him ahead.

Chris's legs felt numb now, as if their blood supply had been cut off, and he couldn't catch his breath, but he kept going, putting one foot in front of the other, concentrating on what he was holding in his arms. "We're doing okay, Molly," he said to her.

He could feel her ribs through her shirt as she breathed in and out in quick puffs.

"Want me to take her?" Pat said.

"Not yet," Chris said. "In a minute, maybe." He'd give Pat a chance to conserve some of his strength. He might need it.

They were across the yard now, cutting between houses again, and Chris could see the street—the big, wide street. Palm was just in front of them. A few feet to Chris's left, an old lady pressed her face against the screen of her front porch as they raced by. For an instant, Chris wondered what she thought, but then they were at the sidewalk, at the street, and he had other things to think about.

Without hesitating, Pat veered right, heading north, and Chris followed him. Sweat was in his eyes, blurring his vision, and he blinked to see—to find what was waiting for them, but he didn't notice anything. Only one car was on the street, and it was moving away from them, toward downtown. "Where is he?" Chris said between breaths. "Where could he be?"

Pat put a hand on Chris's elbow, guiding him off the sidewalk and into the street. "Get a better look at the cross streets out here," Pat said.

"If we don't get run over," Chris said.

"No traffic," Pat said.

Pat was right. The street was definitely empty.

Chris wished there were some cars. Maybe somebody would get curious and stop. But the town wasn't awake yet. They'd already run past a drive-in restaurant and a souvenir shop, and both of them were closed tight.

The first intersection was deserted—no cars and no ice cream trucks—and for a moment Chris dared to think that maybe Bud had taken off for home. They were halfway to the next one when Pat suddenly slowed to a jog. "Give her to me," he said, holding out his arms.

Chris glanced at Pat's face, and then ahead. At the next cross street, a white truck was inching out onto Palm from the right side of the intersection. Bud *hadn't* gone home. "Patty's gonna carry you for a minute, Molly," Chris said, handing her over. He hated to let her go, but he was out of gas, and his arms felt like rubber—it was time for Pat to have her. She went to him without complaining, clinging to his chest and neck like a baby monkey, while he supported her weight with one arm.

"I don't know what Bud's gonna do," Pat said, "but we need to get around him. You might have to distract him or something, Chris." Pat took off again, accelerating up the middle of the street.

Chris caught up to him, and they were running side by side, watching the truck creep farther and farther into the intersection. *Distract him or some-*

*thing,* Chris thought, staring right at the big ice cream cone. They were less than a hundred yards away now. Suddenly the van stopped; the door opened. Bud got out and walked slowly, deliberately, toward them, leaving his truck in the middle of the street. Chris could see a smile now—a forced, counterfeit smile.

"Chris! Pat!" Bud shouted. "Let's talk!" He stopped, ducking down in a half-crouch, his arms at his sides.

"Keep going," Pat said.

Chris didn't have to be told. He was just waiting for Pat to choose a direction. Instead, Pat kept running straight, right at Bud. "What are you doing?" Chris gasped. They were only fifty feet from Bud now.

"Left!" Pat grunted, suddenly veering toward the space between the front of the truck and the curb. Chris planted his right foot to follow him, but his ankle turned and his tired legs couldn't compensate. He went down in a heap, skidding along the pavement. Stunned, his knees and elbows skinned, he lay there for an instant before looking up. When he did, he saw Bud running, trying to cut Pat off before he and Molly could get around the truck. Pat had Molly cradled on his arm like a football, and somehow he had enough stamina to put on a burst of speed, sprinting for the opening. But Bud didn't have as far to go, and he had the angle; he got there first.

Chris watched, getting to his feet as Pat slowed. Chris had to get to them; he had to help. But Pat didn't wait. Three strides away from Bud, he faked right—smooth and quick—and Bud went for it, lunging to his left, grabbing at air, and stumbling to the ground. Pat shifted back, high-stepping it through the gap where Bud had stood an instant before. Chris watched him sprint down the street, and then followed him as fast as he could, skirting around Bud, who was still on the ground, barely moving.

"Molly," he groaned as Chris lurched by.

Pat slowed down, and Chris caught up with him a block from the police station. Chris had checked over his shoulder three times, and Bud hadn't moved. The last time Chris looked, a police car had stopped in front of the truck, its lights flashing.

"Where were you, Kis?" Molly said. She looked worried, but with the pain in his ankle and knees and arms, and the sweat in his eyes, Chris had a hard time focusing on her—especially since her head was bobbing up and down against Pat's shoulder.

He reached over and touched her hair and face, giving her cheek a gentle pinch. He had to make sure she was real—that they really had her.

"Yeah, where were you, Chris?" Pat said. He sounded tired, hoarse, but excited at the same time. His feet half-shuffled, half-plodded along the street, and then the sidewalk.

"I was distracting him," Chris said. He could breathe a little better now. The air was still hot—still sticky—but so what?

"Good job," Pat said.

"He's still back there," Chris said. "There's a police car there now."

"I saw it," Pat said. "Do you think we should go back? He could get away."

"Let's get Molly somewhere safe first. Then we'll worry about him."

An older couple out for a morning walk stopped in their tracks, wide-eyed, as Chris and Pat staggered up to the town hall. The boys were both dirty and sweaty and out of breath, and Chris's elbows and knees were scraped and bleeding. But he didn't even notice. He took Molly from Pat, who opened the door marked POLICE. Chris let out a long breath—more breath than he thought he had—and holding Molly tight to his chest, followed Pat inside.

**20**

A young woman in a gray uniform looked up from behind her desk as Chris and Pat stumbled in. She rose quickly and moved toward them. "Is she all right?" she asked. Molly turned and gave her a shy smile. The woman smiled back at her. "Can I help you kids?" she said.

"This is my sister, Molly," said Chris. "She was kidnapped—by Bud and Clover Butler. We just got her back." He waited.

The woman stared at Chris and gave him a half smile, as if expecting the punch line of a joke. But there was no punch line, and when she looked from Chris to Pat to Molly, her expression changed. "Really?" she said, but she was already moving toward the phone on her desk.

"Bud's just up the street—up Palm—with his ice cream truck," Pat said. "There's a police car there now."

"Blocking the road?" she asked. "The white truck that's blocking the road? The officer just called that one in." She got on the radio, drumming her fingers on the desk while she waited for a response.

"What's goin' on, Lucy?" a voice finally said.

"The ice cream man still there, Sandy?"

"Still here," Sandy said. "Why?"

"Bring him in. He's a kidnap suspect."

The radio buzzed for a moment, then Sandy's voice came on again. "You're talkin' about Bud Butler, Lucy? A kidnap suspect?"

"Affirmative. Treat him as such."

"Will do," Sandy said. "See you in a bit."

"Sit down, you guys," Lucy told them, motioning to a wooden bench across from her desk. They sat, and Chris watched her get on the phone; she grabbed paper and started taking notes. Chris held Molly tightly, not wanting to let go. He was afraid it was all a dream, that he would wake up and find himself in bed, holding his pillow, and she'd be gone. But he could feel her, smell her, see her, and when she looked up at him and smiled, he knew it was real.

"You're squeezin' me, Kis," she said.

"Sorry, Molly." He loved hearing her say his name. He hadn't realized how much he missed it.

"I like it, Kis," she said, and tightened her grip around his neck.

Suddenly, Chris remembered. "Can I use your phone?" he asked Lucy. "I need to call my parents."

"That would be a great idea," she said, "and I need to talk to them, too. Where are they?"

"Wisconsin," Chris said.

*"Wisconsin?* We *are* going to have to listen to your story."

Chris picked up the phone. His fingers were so shaky that he had a hard time pushing the right buttons.

"Hello," a voice said on the other end of the line. It was his dad's voice, but it sounded different: strained, anxious.

"Hi, Dad."

*"Chris—"*

"We've got her, Dad. We've got Molly." He fought down the lump in his throat and waited for his dad to say something.

"Molly?" his dad said finally. His voice was cracking, muffled. "She's alive? She's there with you? *Molly's there with you?"*

Chris heard a click on the other end, and then his mom's voice on the extension. "Chris?" she said, barely whispering. "You've got Molly?"

Chris tried to talk, tried to say yes, but he couldn't get his throat to work. He held Molly closer, feeling her breathe.

"Chris?" his mom said. "Is it really you? Talk to me. Say something to me."

"We've got her, Mom," he said finally.

"She's..." His mom made a noise that sounded as if she was choking, or trying to catch her breath.

"She's fine," he said, giving Molly a squeeze. She was squirming on his lap, reaching for the phone.

"Where are you, Chris?" his dad asked.

"In Florida. We're at the police station in Westview. The town hall, I guess it is."

There was a pause. "Bud and Clover had her?" his dad asked.

"They did," Chris said. He pushed a tear away from his cheek.

"Are you okay? And Pat?"

"We're fine," Chris said. "And Molly wants to talk to you." He handed Molly the phone, helping her hold it up to her ear. Pat hovered over them, smiling, listening. "Say hello to Daddy and Mommy," Chris told Molly.

"Hi, Daddy and Mommy," Molly said. A tiny little voice. Calm. As if she'd last talked to them an hour ago. But Chris could see the light in her eyes. She nodded, answering questions, and Chris had to use his T-shirt to wipe his face. Now that the tears had started, he couldn't turn them off.

"You have to talk, Molly," Chris said. "They can't

see you nodding your head."

"Fine," she said finally, answering some question. Then more nodding. "I missed you, too. I love you, too." Now tears were trickling down Molly's cheeks, streaking her dirt-smudged skin, but Chris let them go. He handed the phone to Lucy.

He felt tired and sore and—all of a sudden—hungry, but he had another feeling that overwhelmed everything else. It was something he couldn't describe, but it warmed him and gave him chills at the same time; it made him happy—beyond happy—but tearful, too. It was a feeling he'd never had before, and somehow doubted he'd ever have again. He buried his face in Molly's hair, wiping away the water from his eyes. She looked at him, a curious expression on her face, and touched him on the cheek.

Lucy showed them to a quiet room, where they ate sandwiches and cookies and listened to voices and noises coming from outside the door. Alone in a big chair, seated across the table from Chris, Molly looked small and vulnerable—too vulnerable. Chris thought of her by herself for all those days and weeks—how frightened and lonely she must have felt—and suddenly the food in his mouth tasted bad. Suddenly he was angry. His hand, wrapped around a pop bottle, grew white-knuckled as he thought about Bud and Clover and how they'd turned Molly's life upside down and broken the hearts of the people who loved her. He forced a smile in Molly's direction and tried to tell himself that everything was okay now. She smiled back at him—a real smile—and he relaxed. He leaned back in the chair and closed his eyes.

□ □ □

It was after dark—nearly 10:30—when Chris's parents arrived at Lucy's house. Chris, Pat, and Molly had spent most of the afternoon and evening napping there; they were wide awake now, peering out the window as a car pulled up. Chris turned Molly toward the door, expecting her to rush to it when it opened, but when his parents hurried in past Lucy and spotted Molly, she hung back bashfully, staring at them from across the room. For a long moment, his parents just stood there looking, as if they were frozen, as if they couldn't believe it was really her. Then his dad pulled his gaze away from Molly and found Chris. It was just a quick glance, but it said everything: concern and relief and thanks and love.

Chris watched his dad's eyes turn liquid as they focused back on Molly and then on Chris's mom. Hand in hand, they started for Molly, inching forward, as if they thought they would scare her off. And then suddenly she was rocketing away from Chris's side, flying to them, and they were down on their knees, hands outstretched, waiting for her. She jumped into their arms and they picked her up, sandwiching her between them, dancing around the room. They were laughing and crying and holding her so close that Chris thought she might be crushed. But her head was tossed back, and she was chuckling—a beautiful, musical sound he'd once thought he'd never hear again.

"Chris! Pat!" his dad shouted. "Get over here. You're not too big for a hug."

But for a long while, Chris just watched; it was a sight he wanted to savor. He glanced at Lucy, still standing by the door, a big smile on her face, and then his eyes blurred over.

Pat walked up beside him and put a hand on his shoulder. "You did it, Chris," he said. "You really did it."

Chris swallowed. "*We,*" he said. "*We* did it, Pat. I couldn't have done it by myself."

They crossed the room to Chris's parents. Chris put his arms around them and closed his eyes. He felt his mom's face, warm and wet against his, and his dad's arm around his shoulders. A small hand on the back of his neck pulled him close, and he could feel Molly's breath, and then her lips, on his cheek. "Are we a family now, Kis?" she asked in his ear. He opened his eyes, looking at her face from inches away, drinking it in. "We sure are, Molly," he said.

"Patty's in our family, too," she said, smiling at Pat. She held out her hands and leaned toward him. He caught her and hoisted her high in the air before lowering her slowly back down, stopping when they were nose to nose.

"Thanks, Molly," he said, and wrapped her up in a bear hug.

"We love you guys," Chris's dad said, his voice cracking.

"We've got to thank you somehow," said Chris's mom. Her cheeks were flushed; her eyes blazed with life.

"You don't need to," Chris said. He'd gotten his sister back. And his family.

Pat grinned. "A new Ferrari would probably do it."

# EPILOGUE

CHRIS sat in the back seat with Molly and watched the countryside float by, waited for the river to come into view. And then it was there, sparkling through bare-limbed trees in the afternoon sun. He stared, remembering how he'd hated it for taking Molly, as if it had been some kind of hungry, cold-blooded monster. But now it was just a river again. Maybe not quite the same river as before Molly disappeared, but no longer a monster.

They approached the house, but the car didn't slow.

"Let's go to the park, first," Chris's dad said, as if it hadn't already been decided. The only one not aware of the itinerary for this trip was Molly, who reacted to the announcement by taking Chris's hand and looking longingly at the house as they passed it by.

Chris would have been happy to stop, too, but he knew they'd be back. They just had to take care of some business at the beach. "We'll be coming right back," he told her.

In the past two months, their lives had returned to normal—or nearly normal—but now they needed to tie up some loose ends, as Dr. Wilde had put it. Clover and Bud were locked up, undergoing psychiatric evaluations and awaiting trial, but Dr. Wilde wanted to make sure that any other bad guys—the kind you can't see—were put away, too. She suggested that the four of them go back to the river as soon as they could. She thought it would be the best place for all of them—especially Molly—to put an end to any surviving demons.

The parking lot was deserted when they pulled in. Chris felt uneasy, but he didn't see any demons. Maybe Molly had, though. She had her jaw stuck out and her eyelids screwed down tight. He slid over and put his arm around her; her shoulders were stiff, unmoving. His mom looked back with a reassuring smile, but Molly didn't see it.

His dad glanced at Molly's face and then turned to his window, staring out at the parking lot as if looking for his own bad guys. When he faced back again, Chris saw anger fading from his eyes. "We've got some bread for the ducks, Molly," Chris's dad said, smiling now. "Should we go see if they're hungry?" He took her hand and held on.

Molly opened her eyes and looked around, slowly surveying the lot, looking for—what? Chris wondered. Maybe a big white truck with an ice cream cone on its side. But the only thing she saw was an empty parking lot covered with fallen leaves. And now she had ducks on her mind. Now she was in a hurry.

A minute later they were heading for the beach. Chris hung back, ambling along, taking everything in, remembering the day he'd last been here with Molly. Now that she was back, that day—the whole summer—seemed even more unreal, while today— what was happening right now—was all that was important. He watched her pad down the path in front of him, hurrying toward the water, with her bag of bread in one hand, her dad's hand in the other, and her mom—as close as a shadow—on her other side.

At first, Chris's parents looked like bodyguards, trying to be casual while constantly glancing from Molly to every tree and bush they passed, as if some- thing were about to jump out and snatch her away. But then they seemed to relax, and when she began tugging them along after spotting some ducks in the shallows, they let her run ahead, content to watch her sprint for the shoreline. Suddenly Molly—and her mom and dad—had decided that this place was okay again, that there was nothing left to bother her here.

A cool breeze stirred, quickly draining the warmth from the sunshine, and Chris stopped in his tracks. From somewhere, the sweet autumn fragrance of burning leaves came to him, filling his nose. He closed his eyes and breathed deeply, finding another smell: the river. It smelled fresh now, renewed by rain and wind and cold, crisp nights. He held his breath, not wanting to let it go. He listened to the rattle of swirling leaves slow and then stop as the breeze died. And then his dad's voice, loud and strong, carried to him through the still air.

"Molly!" he called. "Molly!" And for an awful instant, Chris went back, his heart in his throat, to that other day at the river. But then he opened his eyes and saw his dad and mom waving to Molly. His dad had a camera up to his face, trying to get her attention, but she was too busy with the ducks, out of the water now and crowding around her feet, scrambling for bread crumbs. And then she turned, searching for something, for someone.

"Kis!" she shouted, finally spotting him. "Kis!"

He waved and started toward her.

"Kis!" she yelled again. "Hurry! Too many custards! I need your help!"

He smiled, deep inside he smiled, and broke into a jog. In a moment he was sprinting, running over and around rocks and logs and bushes, racing for the shoreline, for Molly.